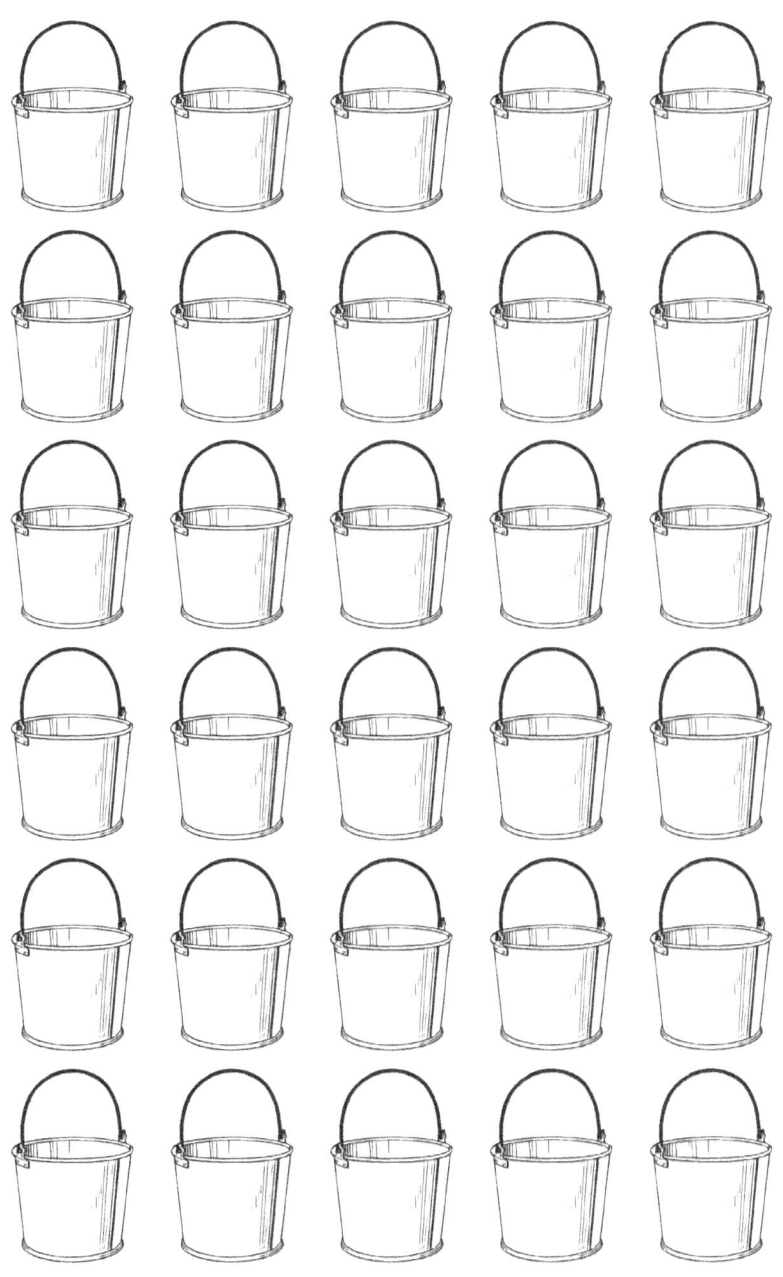

Pure Slush Books

2014
August

Vol. 8

a Pure Slush book

2014 August Vol. 8 is edited by Matt Potter and
published by Pure Slush, June 2014.

Cover photograph: canola field, Meechi Road,
near Langhorne Creek, South Australia
Front cover photograph and design copyright © Matt Potter

ISBN: 978-1-925101-40-9

Find *Pure Slush* at http://pureslush.webs.com

Copies of all *Pure Slush* publications can be bought
at http://pureslush.webs.com/store.htm

All queries re *Pure Slush* can be made
via email to edpureslush@live.com.au

A note on differences in punctuation and spelling

Pure Slush proudly features (both online and in print) writers from all over the English-speaking world. Some speak and write English as their first language, while for others, it's their second or third or even fourth language. Naturally, across all versions of English, there are differences in punctuation and spelling, and even in meaning. These differences are reflected in the stories *Pure Slush* publishes, and it accounts for any differences in punctuation, spelling and meaning found within these pages.

stories by

Guilie Castillo-Oriard

Townsend Walker

Derek Osborne

Gloria Garfunkel

John Wentworth Chapin

Lynn Beighley

Andrew Stancek

Rachel Ambrose

Gill Hoffs

Susan Tepper

Jessica McHugh

Shane Simmons

Michelle Elvy

Len Kuntz

Michael Webb

James Claffey

Gwendolyn Joyce Mintz

Stephen V. Ramey

Gay Degani

Sally-Anne Macomber

Mandy Nicol

Margaret Bingel

Darryl Price

Teresa Burns Gunther

Matt Potter

Gary Percesepe

Nathaniel Tower

Kimberlee Smith

Vanessa Weibler Paris

Joanne Jagoda

h. l. nelson

Friday

1

August
2014

Quixote Always
Loses

by Guilie Castillo-Oriard

The Curaçao branch of Ehrlich Fiduciary operates out of an eighteenth-century *landhuis* that's been declared a World Heritage site. As far as the island government's concerned, this alone justifies outrageous rent – which does not include maintenance. The sprawling plantation house is all high ceilings and French doors and wide verandas and hardwood shutters. The parquet floors, waxed every three months, make the clack of Milena Durant's favorite Jimmy Choos echo through the halls. When she's working late she goes barefoot, which has made her privy to much she shouldn't be. Information is mighty currency.

But the grapevine isn't infallible.

The best view in the building, hands down, is from the south side of Wing B. Milena's office, to be exact. Caribbean blue in sky and sea fills three quarters of the window behind her desk. The riot-colored buildings of the Handelskade – that cupcake Amsterdam, the unofficial icon of this tiny and otherwise unknown island – fill the remaining quarter. A bright cruise ship, Royal Caribbean judging by the size, perches today like overripe fruit in the middle ground.

The view is wasted on the two people in Milena's office. She's paging, somewhat vaguely, through a yellow legal pad. The man sitting across the desk from her, Ehrlich Group CEO Rowan Barry, has turned his chair sideways, and seems deep in contemplation of the shirt buttons straining over the zeppelin of his belly.

"Is this going to be a problem?"

Milena looks up, but he's still gazing at his stomach. A touch of mutiny creeps into her reply. "Why would it?"

He sucks on his lower lip. "You and I don't often clash on judgment issues. I thought you might be ... disappointed."

"Disappointment implies gain was expected. I've nothing to gain from who takes my place. Surprised, yes. Not disappointed."

"He was your hire. You did expect –"

"He was *your* hire, Rowan. Remember? I wanted to hire that ballbreaker from London to replace Stepan as Legal Counsel and make *him* Managing Director. You were the one who insisted on Luis."

"He's Latin. The Mexican market is going to hell. Someone like him, with his connections, his track record, can make all the difference."

"Which explains why I'm surprised."

Rowan taps his thumbs on the tautness of his stomach, a pensive drumroll. "He'll be a great MD. One day. When he's not so raw. So full of –" He tilts back the granite block of his head, looks for the word he wants – which, apparently, isn't *shit* – in the ceiling beams. "Idealism. Pipe dreams. You know what I mean. You were, too, at one point."

"So were you. All of us."

He looks at her. "An MD can't be a Quixote."

"He'll grow out of it. We all –"

"I have ample faith he will. What I'm saying – what Group is saying – is not *yet*. You need to name your successor. You need to begin the transition. Stepan is chomping at the bit to get started."

Milena leans back, and her chair creaks a complaint. "You spoke to Stepan? Already?"

"We had to know if he was on board." Rowan's lids droop to half-mast.

Why did she think there was still a chance, that her window – Luis's window – was still open? "He'll leave, you know."

Rowan uses the corner of a post-it pad to clean under the nail of his thumb. "He's bluffing."

"It's the only reason he came here. To be MD. He'll have nothing to stay for." And he'll blame her. He'll think it's because of that stupid fight. Her tantrum over that woman. He'll think she's punishing him. Which wouldn't be so farfetched if it was anyone else.

Her mother defined love as wishing for someone else's happiness more than you wish for your own. Over the last month, Milena has had to come to terms with the fact she might be – no, is – in love. The worst kind.

The kind without a future. (She's leaving, Luis is staying.)

The unrequited kind. (She's no naïf.)

The kind where none of the above makes a whit of difference.

And the only thing she has to give that might have any value at all to him – her current job – isn't, it's been decided, hers to give.

Rowan rests an elbow on the desk. "Luis wants to leave, let him. But I'll bet you next year's NOPAT he won't. I'll bet you this year's *and* next year's."

"What if he does, Rowan?"

"He's too proud. How would he explain leaving Cabrera y Machado in Mexico City for this nine-month stint in the Caribbean? He won't be happy, sure, but he'll finish his contract."

"And if you're wrong? Are we willing to lose him?"

He studies her with those half-lidded eyes. Frog eyes. Cold eyes. "Are you? How far would you go to avoid losing him? If this were your call, would you hand over this office – *your* office – to Luis? Now?"

Luis, who still cares so much about Doing The Right Thing. Luis, who refuses to grasp the basic give-and-take that keeps this business running. Luis, who has no guile in his soul – not even enough to realize how transparent his Man Of The World act is. Luis, who expects the world to function according to karmic rules or something. Being completely objective, all emotion aside, all personal involvement – even if objectivity isn't something she feels capable of right now – there can only be one answer.

"No," she says, and the guilt feels like the Devil whispering in her ear.

"Good." Rowan stands, stretches. Nonchalant. Heedless of the lives lying in shards around him. "Look into that replacement for Stepan, will you? The – what did you call her? The ballbreaker?"

"She's with Ernst & Young now. Legal for LatAm. We'd have to offer her diamonds and pearls to get her here."

"Would she consider MD in a couple of years? Stepan wants to go to Luxembourg. You know he turned down Singapore? Said he's had it with tropical weather."

Her stomach turns a triple axel, lands wrong, doesn't quite recover. "What about Luis?"

Rowan shrugs. "A little competition won't hurt him. Might even help him."

Luis will hate – no, revile her. But that won't be as bad as knowing the damage she's inflicted on his career. Because her fucking him did, in fact, fuck him over. If she hadn't been sleeping with him, she'd have made damn sure he was ready. Instead, she coddled him. Didn't push hard enough. Didn't coach him the way she should have. Not in the office, anyway.

Perhaps she can still help him. Not that he'll ever know, or believe it if he did. "I agree, Rowan, that Luis isn't ready now. But he'll be a kick-ass MD one day, not too far in the future. Ehrlich would do well to make sure he doesn't leave us before then."

Rowan acknowledges that with a single nod. "Sounds good. But at what price, Milena?"

"Forget about that London woman. It won't work, and she'll be ridiculously expensive. Wasn't the Brazil Legal Counsel looking to relocate? He knows Stepan. They'd work well together." And with his Compliance background, Milena feels he's unlikely to have MD ambitions. He won't be a rival for Luis.

"It's an option."

"A good option. It'll make it easier to convince Luis of staying."

Rowan nods again, noncommittally, and turns to go. That's it, that's all the assurance she'll get. Now she has to find a way – and the balls – to break it to Luis.

With a hand on the door, Rowan turns back. "What about Singapore?"

"What about it?"

"The Latin American market, especially the Mexican market, has strong ties there. Treaties and such. Lots of opportunities. Something to consider, perhaps."

Milena feels cold creeping up to her face. "You mean – Luis should go in my stead?"

Rowan chuckles, dry as winter-chapped lips. "I don't want him running a branch, but you think I'll give him a position in Group? No, Milena. I meant a – I don't know, a directorship or something. Get him to run a few projects, get him involved with sales maybe. Or he could work with Asian clients. Something new for him."

"He knows Asian clients. He was in Hong Kong for two years with HSBC." Her head is spinning.

"Just an idea, Milena." He winks at her, opens the door. "You could come up with something interesting for him there. If you wanted to."

Rowan, the bastard, always manages to find that most secret hope: one's most contemptible temptation. And then he holds it out, a careless child squeezing a baby chick, daring you to do something, anything, before he squashes it to death.

Typical Rowan, the bastard. Find that most secret of hopes, then go for its jugular.

Saturday

2

August
2014

La Ronde /
Jimmie and Sal

by Townsend Walker

The phone rings in Jimmie's Bungalow in Venice Beach. It's Sal.

"Jimmie, sweetheart, how's the leg?"

"How the fuck you think it is?"

"I heard you broke it."

"Heard I broke it? What are you, some kind of pathological sadist?"

"Jimmie, Jimmie, let me explain things to you. I had to do that, had to."

"No, I don't understand why you had to break my leg."

"But, since I like you, it was a clean break, no? It'll heal quick. I even asked this doc I know what kind of break heals best, and my guys called 911, didn't they. That's the kind of friend I am."

"Sal, you have so missed the point, I don't believe it. Why did you <u>have</u> to break my leg?"

"I thought you knew. You have some time?"

"That's all I got these days."

"I lend you money. You don't pay me back. I ask and ask. You don't pay me back. If word gets out that there are no consequences when Salvatore Mancuso doesn't get paid back, what kind of business is he running? You see?"

"But you were an investor, you were an owner. I didn't borrow money, you invested in a movie production. Big difference."

"You said, and I remember things like this, you said 'Sal, my friend, I have this fantastic script, if the Weinsteins or MGM knew, they'd snap it up in a minute. But I'm giving you this opportunity. I want you to think about it as a loan with a guaranteed interest rate of 1000%."

"That's the way we pitch out here. Where you been?"

"Well where I been is that if you don't come up with something by the end of this week you're going to need a wheelchair, not crutches my friend."

"Look, I got this opportunity for you to cash in big time, say $150-200K."

"Opportunity? Sounds like I gotta do something to get my money. Not exactly precisely how this business works."

"Well, you wanna hear about it or not?"

"How much you say?"

"150-200K."

"Speak to me."

"This dame in Manhattan, Park Avenue, is paying to off her husband cuz he beats her up."

"You need a hit man. Me, I'm a money man. I lend money. I take risks most banks wouldn't even let walk in the door, much less open your mouth. What do I know about hit men? I run a legitimate business activity."

"Okay, okay. I just thought maybe this was a way I could pay you back."

"Jimmie baby, I gotta run, call you back, maybe I'll drop by later. You gonna be there?"

"Where the fuck you think I'm going with a busted leg? Clubbing? I don't think so, and you wouldn't believe how unfashionably shaped and colored casts are. I wouldn't be seen outside with it."

Jimmie hobbles into the kitchen to make a sandwich, opens a bottle of Grey Riesling to wash it down, goes out to the pool with the bottle (no glass) and a ham sandwich. Thinks to himself: awful look tan line I'm going to have with this cast. Then:

"Damn him to hell," to himself.

"Damn him to hell," louder.

"Damn him to hell," to the sidewalk.

The gate opens, the Sal-your-pal demeanor is on display: wide grin on a broad face, kind blue eyes, ruddy cheeks, blond hair slicked back. Sal has a square head sitting on a square body, tailored suits that make him nearly (stress on nearly) suave. Today he's sporting a tan suit, Super 200 wool.

"Who you damning to hell in here?"

"Oh, it's you. No one, no one, just aggravated by this fucking leg."

"Well, to show you where my heart is I brought you some flowers. Roses, sent up from Ecuador, this guy says. You imagine that, sending flowers on a plane all the way from Ecuador. That's got to be what, 5000 miles?"

"Well, maybe three. You want some wine? There's another bottle in the fridge. Glasses are in the cupboard."

Sal comes back out from the kitchen with two glasses and wine in an ice bucket. And some roasted almonds.

"The living room, what are you starting up, a bordello? All that velvet and wood."

"Nah, friend of mine, decorator, experimenting with stuff. I said he could use it."

Sal flops down in a lounge chair next to Jimmie; claps him on the leg.

"Shit!"

"Sorry, didn't notice. That's the bad one, huh?"

Under his breath: "This will pass. This will pass. This will pass."

"I made some inquiries."

"And?"

"We can probably do business, but you gotta understand, there's a fifty percent discount on whatever the dame pays."

"Fifty fucking percent?"

"What can I say? Standard. You want me to break the rules of the game. No, of course you don't."

"Like I have a choice."

"That's the spirit, my friend."

Sal moves closer to Jimmie and whispers. *"Now you tell me everything I need to know to find this guy and the dame with the money."*

"The guy's name is Franklin Lincoln Cabot III."

"So what's he look like?"

"Big guy: six foot, maybe a little less, 250, pasty faced, big nose, curly hair."

"What color?"

"Black, I think."

"You think? What's he do?"

"Gotta get back to you on that one?"

"Excuse me. You gotta get back to me? Did I hear that right? You, who are giving me this gift to pay back what you owe me? You do have some idea of how many people there are in Manhattan?"

"Yeah, yeah. I know."

"What else do you know?"

"He wears blue tinted Prada aviators, rain, snow and shine and he loses his kids in the park."

"Well now Jimmie my lad, you haven't told me jack-all. I'd suggest you get more information before I even want to think about accepting this job as partial payment for what you owe. Capice?"

"Yeah, I understand, Sal. I'll get back to you, tonight, promise."

"While you're at it. How about the name of the dame who's making the payoff? I'll leave you now to go to work."

"Sure, tonight, promise."

On his way out Sal raps Jimmie's cast with the butt end of his pistol.

"Sayonara, sweetheart."

Under his breath, "Fuck you."

Jimmie hustles to his computer looking for Cabot. Not hard to find, works at the Goldman, had a society wedding. Photos of Frank and Madge at benefit functions. Jimmie pays (not insignificant amounts) for phone numbers and addresses.

Three hours later.

"Sal, Jimmie. Here's the scoop."

"Let's hope you got it right this time. You got a lot riding on it."

Things We Can't Explain

by Derek Osborne

Max had never asked God for anything, he never felt he had the right, not during the war, nor that night off Hatteras when he was sure the sea would take them, not even when Maggie lay dying. But that day as he watched the Dock Master beating Rebecca's chest, the Coast Guard EMT's opening their packs, the smell of oxygen – he prayed – it wasn't their time. Leaning against the companionway ladder he had closed his eyes and pleaded and begged and promised he'd do anything, anything so long as they lived.

And so they did.

"I wasn't sure about the color," he says, looking about the room they've converted for Rebecca's recovery. It's the house he and Eddie went to look at that July 3rd morning. Rebecca spent nearly a month in Boston General. They flew her back to Nantucket earlier this week. The room they've set up was originally an enclosed sun-porch off the back deck, a sweeping view of the harbor, but now it's equipped with a hospital bed, a nightstand, a small sitting area with an entertainment unit and a big brass telescope. Max is hoping the telescope will give Rebecca something to do, satisfy her natural curiosity, *snooping*, la senora would say. It will be her place for the next three months. From the porch they can see the entire harbor and most of the waterfront. The break in her fibula (the sudden crack that loosed the tiny fragment of bone which travelled up to her heart) will need at least six more weeks to heal. She had been without breath for less than four minutes. By all accounts the baby is fine. It's a hot August morning; at least there's a breeze.

"It is very nice," Rebecca says, though he knows she's being polite. She can only take a mild pain suppressant due to the pregnancy. Max has broken his share of bones and he knows the discomfort. Anja's doing a terrific job with massage oils and flower essences and every homeopathic remedy in the book. Eddie comes by in the afternoons and plays his guitar. They've flown in an acupressure specialist. Max doesn't care what it costs.

La senora turns her nose up at most of it, though she did gave Anja a check, in secret. "If all that nonsense helps so be it," she said at dinner, and then, when she and Max were alone, "This is not your fault. She's been getting hurt like this ever since she was small. A regular tomboy." It's interesting how her English becomes quite good when they're alone.

"And how are you?" Rebecca is asking. It's not hard to see how much the past few weeks have taken out of him. The cancer is spreading.

"I'm fine."

"Liar."

"I am. I have everything I've ever wanted."

He's forgotten Andi is sitting in the other room. Rebecca glances in her direction.

"You two still need to talk," she says, "This has all got to be very hard for her."

Andi is pretending she can't hear. The painted gray floorboards and windowed walls bounce the sound like a drum.

"Andi," Rebecca says, "can you please come here for a moment?"

Max has been avoiding this ever since that day in the hospital, the day he got confused. He's watching his daughter walk across the room. She glides, like her mother did. Maggie studied dance when she and Max were in school. Grace seems to have come naturally to their youngest.

"Give me your hand," Rebecca says.

The air is still ionized from the morning squalls. All of the French doors along the porch are open, the sun rushing in. It's Sunday, the boats out in the harbor are leaving and some have their sails set; less experienced owners stay under power. The big mega-yachts won't go until after lunch. For them, Newport is only an hour or two away.

"I've ordered a motorized chair," Max says, indicating the telescope. "It will lift you up to the eyepiece ..."

"Max," Rebecca says.

He looks at his daughter, taking a deep breath.

"Guys, I'm okay," she says, but the tears are already coming. "I am."

Max is standing on the other side of the bed. He comes around. At 5 ft 4 she barely comes up to his chest.

Rebecca is still holding her hand. She looks up at Max. "I am not," she says, matter of fact, speaking to Andi. "I have just met the love of my life and now I am going to lose him. My baby will never know his father."

Max has closed his eyes, slowly shaking his head. He's never been good with these things.

"I'm just so angry!" Andi says, breaking away and stepping back toward the open doors.

Max knows what is coming next. He can see his daughter looking around. She has always had a habit of throwing things.

"Not the telescope!"

She had indeed been eyeing the scope, but instead grabs the spindle back chair beside it and in one fluid motion has it over her head, coming down in a slanting arc and catching the edge of the open door beyond. The chair and the glass explode as she falls to her knees. La senora comes rushing in. Max raises his hand to her to stop.

"I'm just so angry," Andi says, fists clenched, emphasizing the word. "I know Mom's been dead almost eight years but shouldn't I hate you? (This to Rebecca) Shouldn't I be pissed at both of you? (Then at Max) You've acted like two spoiled brats with no concern for anyone … like children … like …"

"Like people in love?" la senora says from the doorway. "As if there will be no tomorrow."

"Fuck it," Andi screams, bringing her fists to the floor. She is still kneeling among the splinters and glass. She does not mean la senora, more like she is cursing the room, the house, the island, as if her screams might be heard by everyone, everywhere.

"Max, give her a pillow."

Max grabs one of the pillows from the bed and shoves it underneath his daughter just as she comes down again but it's too late. They all hear the crush.

"Fuck you," she growls, raising her fists again and bringing them down again on the pillow this time. "Fuck you."

The pillow is bloody.

"Go on," Rebecca says, practically cheering her on, "Beat them all. Beat them for me."

Eddie and Anja have come into the room.

"Smash them to pieces," Anja says.

All Eddie sees is the blood and the screaming.

And Andi is really screaming, "Fuck you! fuck you!" and flailing at will. She growls like a dog. The pillow is starting to tear. Max is trying to gauge the extent of her cuts as she lifts and pounds the pillows. He decides it can wait. The others have circled around his daughter there in front of the bed.

"It's not fair," Rebecca says, raising her voice.

"It's not," Andi says.

"It's just not fair!" Rebecca yells.

Max wants to run from the room. By the look on Eddie's face, he's thinking the same thing.

"Fuck it," Andi says, bringing both her fists down again.

"Fuck it," Anja blurts out.

"Fuck it," the three of them say in unison as Andi starts swinging her clenched fists like a club.

"Fuck it," the three of them say again.

It's becoming a chant. "Fuck it … Fuck it … Fuck it … Fuck … It … Fuck … Fuck …" Andi is getting tired but doesn't quit. She doesn't see the blood. The pillow has long since died, its guts spilling out over the boards. She's pounding a bloody corpse. "Fuck it," she says, now out of breath, barely able to talk. "Fuck it." With one final effort she rises, bringing her open hands up over her head, collapsing over what's left of the pillow. "Fuck it," she whispers, eyes closed, completely exhausted.

Max looks up at Rebecca. She's crying but also glaring, indicating their daughter. In that moment, this is suddenly how he thinks of her, their daughter, he sits down on the floor beside her – the glass is everywhere – and gathers her into his arms.

"Daddy, please don't go."

For the first time in his life, Max cannot fix this. He looks up again at Rebecca. In less than six months they have lived a lifetime. He remembers, they both remember, that first night on the boat. He had told her he wouldn't. He was sure then he would beat it. Eddie and Anja are holding each other. There's this look on Eddie's face; it's finally sinking in.

"I think we should all get married on Labor Day," he says, surprising even himself.

Andi looks up as if he's gone mad.

"I agree," la senora says. "It will be a beautiful double wedding."

"Oh god," Rebecca says in her best Brooklyn accent.

"I will see to everything," la senora adds. "And tonight I am cooking paella."

The Dread of the Jewish High Holidays

by Gloria Garfunkel

Ralph here. I forced myself to go to the Cape with Chloe for two weeks. My boss at Orwellian balked about the short notice and so I told him I'm so stressed out he can chalk it up to sick time. I'm covered by the Americans with Disabilities Act. They all know I'm bipolar anyway, it's obvious, and they can't fire me for it. They have to make reasonable accommodations, so fuck them. I drag myself into work bolstered by vats of caffeine no matter how bad I feel. I deserve this break.

The ocean and long walks on sand mellow me out, waves of peace washing over me as I lie on the sunny beach. There's a cool breeze but the sun is hot. Nirvana. This is how I feel when I'm stable, except for a little bit of irritability and dread when it gets dark.

As the days are getting shorter, I try not to think about the Jewish holidays in the fall, having to beg God to let you live another year and being held accountable for all your sins on Rosh Hashanah and Yom Kippur and the ten days in between. What a fucking depressing religion. I often just want to pray to God to strike me down dead right there and get it over with. I hate having to beg for my life every year, especially when I'm depressed and not sure I want it.

The biggest problem with bipolar is that you spend most of it miserable and only a very tiny smidgen of it euphoric which you lie to your doctor doesn't exist because you don't want her to medicate it but your fast speech and "flight of ideas" give you away every time and up goes the dose of Lithium to smack you down to bland.

I'm lucky that Chloe is so tolerant of my moods. I think I'd be dead already without her. But I'd never do that to her. She's the best part of my life. She brings me peace, whenever possible.

Tuesday

5

August
2014

Mauve

by John Wentworth Chapin

The woman in front of Charles argues fiercely: "My father was the greatest man *on the planet*, and no one *ever* … my *mother* didn't even appreciate him. He was a *great* man." She shouts this at the bowl of mashed potatoes and plastic tumbler of iced tea on her cafeteria tray. They do not argue back.

This has been going on for several minutes. Charles lifts his own tray off the rails and maneuvers around her, heading for the salad bar and the desserts.

"Hey. HEY! No cutting."

Charles turns; Mashed Potato Lady stands frozen, both hands clutching her tray, dark eyes glaring in his direction under furrowed brows.

"I didn't *cut*," Charles corrects her. "I passed you."

"YOU CUT! You were behind me, and YOU GOTTA WAIT YOUR TURN."

The buzzing chatter of mealtime has quieted around them. Mashed Potato Lady's feet are planted firmly: dingy pink espadrilles with raveling hemp soles.

"You were having an important conversation. With your food. I didn't want to interrupt, so I went around you," Charles says, quietly.

MPL shouts again. "YOU CAN'T CUT. Everyone hasta wait their turn."

Flecks of amethyst spittle sparkle in the institutional glare. A week ago, he would have resigned himself to trotting back in line behind MPL, but there's only so much grinning and bearing that Charles can take.

Charles goads the woman. "Everyone's father is a fucking asshole." He narrows his eyes at her – don't fuck with me, the eyes say. "Pull it together," he hisses and turns back to the salad bar.

"You can't *cut*," he hears her grumble.

Then she's silent: she is mollified.

Good job, Charles tells himself. His therapist advised him to recognize his feelings and he is doing it –

Something wet and heavy hits Charles' shoulder and neck, then drops to the floor. Charles knows it's mashed potatoes; at his feet, a melamine bowl clanks to a rest.

The room is now silent. He turns to find MPL scowling at him from the same spot, lightened tray wobbling in one hand. Charles sees options:

a.   take the high road: apologize and move back behind her

b.   take the tolerable high road: turn back around and ignore her

c.   take the middle road: scrape the mashed potatoes off his t-shirt and fling it in her general direction

d.   escalate this motherfucker

He drops his tray on the rail and walks the few steps in MPL's glowering direction. They are the same height, so he gets face to face. He says, "I am not about to put up with your *shit*." He takes the tumbler of iced tea from her tray and pours it on her head. The liquid is a deep, rich purple: grape juice, not iced tea as it seemed.

She sputters and wipes her face with one hand. "You're a cutter!" she shrieks. She whacks Charles with her tray, a firm two-handed tennis backhand. He deflects it with his forearm, glaring at her juice-streaked eyes; the tray falls to the linoleum.

"You're a fucking crazy person!" he barks, and as she reaches to claw at his throat, a pair of young staff members wearing St. Bernice's institutional violet polo shirts jog toward them across the linoleum.

The lavender walls blend into windows filled with a late evening sky.

"We don't use the word *crazy* at St. Bernice's," the therapist says. She's one of many; he doesn't think he's seen the same one twice.

Charles says, "I suppose we don't throw mashed potatoes, either."

"You're responsible for your own actions," she said.

She's aggravatingly robotic. He shoots back, "How would you *like* me to have responded?"

"How would you like to have responded?"

"Exactly as I did, except I wouldn't have slipped on the grape juice," he answers. His tailbone is killing him. For this and a multitude of reasons, Charles wishes he'd chosen pills over booze. Drinkers are unkempt, unsteady, unpleasant, unresponsive: they're just nasty. It's like bunking with the homeless. Pills would have given him a higher-class environment. He didn't even realize until after he'd admitted himself that there are residential programs for eating disorders and internet addictions. *Way* better.

She doesn't accept his answer. "What would have happened ... if you turned the other cheek?" She says this more like it's a quiz than a question. Clearly, there's a right answer.

"It was unkind of me to call her crazy," Charles admits. "But she threw food at me and she was out of control."

"So you felt it was your job to teach her a lesson."

34

"She threw mashed potatoes at me!"

"If she fell and got mashed potatoes all over you by mistake, what would you have done?" The therapist waits a moment, but Charles doesn't respond. "You probably would've helped her up, right? Same outcome, different response. She bruised your ego and you retaliated, Charles. It triggered you. Until you see that, you will be a marionette, jerking and dancing."

"So I should just let people walk all over me?"

The therapist sighs, disengaged. "We don't have space for people who interfere with other residents' treatment. Delaney seems to think you were insulting her father. I don't think you appreciate the greater implications of your actions here, in this facility. You are restricted from the cafeteria. We can reassess in two days."

The cafeteria is nasty, but he doesn't like being punished; it's a matter of pride. "I don't belong here," he says.

The therapist nods. "You are welcome to leave at any time."

Charles says, "No, you don't understand. I'm not an alcoholic."

The therapist touches the folder again, almost longingly. He can see that she wants him to leave. "If you don't belong, why are you here?" she asks.

"I know that's an alcoholic cliché, right? But I just want you to know that it's true. I quit my job and I admitted myself to this place because … I thought I needed a reset. To get away for a bit."

"You checked yourself into St Bernice's as a vacation." The therapist looks around her at the relentless, sad, institutional lavender.

"I didn't do my research very well," Charles admits. "This was the wrong place. Plus, I hated my job."

"I don't think it requires a whole lot of wisdom to recognize that when you find yourself in the wrong place, you should leave." She closes a lavender folder that matches the walls.

Charles says, "You mean the job? Or you mean you're throwing me out of rehab?"

"I was in rehab until this afternoon," Charles says to the bartender. He chews the cherry from his third supergay cocktail.

"Rehab sucks," she answers.

Charles nods. "I didn't really belong there."

"It worked for me, I mean," she says. "I took pills. Three weeks in rehab and never looked back."

Charles says, "I went because I thought being with more fucked-up people than myself might be enlightening. It was just crappy." Charles studies her; she isn't very high-class clientele. He thinks he might have been wrong about wishing for pill rehab.

"Maybe you'll go back when you're ready," the bartender says, shrugging. She slides a vodka with grapefruit juice and cranberry seltzer in front of him and he takes a sip. An older woman two stools down has been punching buttons on her phone and squinting at the screen in the dim lighting. She leans across the empty stool and taps Charles on the forearm.

"You're not supposed to tell a bartender you just got out of rehab while you order a drink," she whispers, overly loud. Charles doesn't respond, but she winks, and he realizes it's a joke. He also knows it was meant as a joke because she is laughing and Charles and the bartender aren't.

"Good point," he says. He hoists his glass to the woman and she leans across to clink cocktails. It's dim in here, but the woman's garish clothes – is she really wearing a purple and magenta paisley caftan? – light her up like Vegas.

"I can tell you're not a drinker. Anyone who drinks knows to stay away from the grapefruit juice," the woman says. "It'll tear your stomach up before you can crawl in your car and get a DWI."

Another joke unlaughed at by Charles and the bartender.

"I like your bracelet," she says, pointing at his wrist.

"I got it in India a few months ago," he said. It is a cheap stretchy thing with little squares of polished coconut shell. "I think it looks like shiny chunks of Toblerone."

The woman laughs harder than the comment deserves and slaps the back of the empty stool. "I like you," she announces, to the bar in general. "My name's Deonna. How would you like a job?"

Now, *this*, thinks Charles, is crazy.

Unmended Fences

by Lynn Beighley

My dad is twitchy. We've managed to get out without a camera pointed at me, and yet he's nervous. What is he up to?

"What are you up to, Dad?"

"Uh, well ..."

Crap, there is something with which he is up to with. Something like that. Last time, it was letting the *You Tell Me* people film me in bed. Could this be worse than that?

And it seems like every time I'm in a restaurant, something horrible happens. God, it's true. First, Bill Plover fell in love with me, then I went out with him because America told him to and because I'm an idiot, then we went out again because I wanted money and he tried to propose, then Seamus asked me out but set me up to run into Bill because he wanted money. I look around for the cameras or Bill. Or Seamus. Nope. Just my dad.

"Princess ..." he says.

Yes, this is going to be bad. I grip the edge of my chair and wait for it.

"The thing is, I've fallen in love. I've asked her to marry me and she's said yes."

Oh. Well, that's not so bad. I look around for the cameras again, but I start to relax while he raves about his beloved. Maybe this time it'll be a nice dinner.

Here's the summary:

1. Her name is Gloria. She's a widow. He met her online a month ago.

2. She's a vegan nudist who enjoys taxidermy and snowboarding (presumably while dressed).

3. They are IN LOVE and don't see any reason to wait.

And I'm smiling. Dad is glowing. He tells me she's going to join us in a few minutes. I don't see a downside. He's happy, she can't be in it for his money, because he doesn't have any, and maybe with him involved in his own life, he'll stay out of mine.

He's sitting up straight, now, the nervousness gone. He orders a bottle of champagne and a dozen oysters. Which I'll be paying for.

"JENNNNNNN!" Someone is shrieking. Arms grab me from behind and wrap around me like tentacles.

And she's here. She releases me and I turn. Dad introduces us, although there's no reason for him to. I get my first look at her.

She's cute. And she's taken care of herself. Maybe a bit overcoiffed, with puffy blonde hair. Killer tan (but well, nudist, I guess she gets a fair bit of sun). She looks sane. And in spite of her enthusiastic mauling of me, she seems quite nice.

We sit and talk as the champagne arrives. I'm relaxed in a way that I haven't been in six months. Now that the whole *You Tell Me* crap is over, maybe life can get back to normal. Or even better than normal.

"Jenn, we're so happy you'll help us out like this," Gloria gushes.

"I just want to see Dad happy, Gloria." I'm a bit perplexed by the word "help".

"Pookie, see? You had nothing to worry about!"

"Uh, I didn't ask her yet, Honeybear," Dad mumbles, looking down. Dad's face turns red.

"What? Just say it."

It comes out in a mumbled rush. "Bill, your Bill's my

best man. Because we get a free wedding and honeymoon out of it."

I can't speak. I reach in my bag and start digging around for some cash. Gloria starts chattering.

"And you're my maid of honor, Jenn! I have such a gorgeous dress all picked out for you."

I spit out, "hell no." I throw a handful of cash on the table and leave.

I'm not sure how I manage to make my way to my apartment building, but I do. I collapse on my couch.

I guess I've slept, because it's dark. My doorbell is ringing.

"GO AWAY DAD," I yell. But the doorbell keeps ringing. I go to the door and I jerk it open.

It's Seamus. That bastard.

He's holding a bouquet of what looks like weeds (complete with dandelions). Stands there, shoulders slumped, the dimple on his left cheek nowhere in evidence.

"Jenn, God. I'm such a dick. You have to forgive me."

I grab his arm and pull him in, and then I pull him even closer. He drops the flowers as he wraps his arms around me in a hug I hope never ends.

Vtak Ohnivak

by Andrew Stancek

They say the whole house went up in a flash. The bombs at Hiroshima and Nagasaki evaporated matter, nothing left, and this sounds something like that. This is my neighborhood and I remember the house. I've been to Hank Johnson's parties on this street and I helped put out a fire, an ordinary kitchen grease fire, three doors down, some years back.

An ordinary lower middle-class suburb, fields at the north end and a mixed, poorer neighborhood at the other. No more crime than anywhere in America today, unexceptional in every way. No famous sons and no national headlines until now.

I studied chemistry in college. I understand fire, causes, accelerants and retardants. Fire is my life, you could say, and I'm fascinated by it. I've set fires and I've put them out. I paid my dues, started part-time like everybody, but was good enough to get promoted to a full-time firefighter job, and if I'd carried on, would have had a good shot at becoming Chief. Now I earn every penny the insurance company pays me, save them a fortune, you need a logical, disciplined mind and the ability to sniff something wrong if you're an investigator, and I am damn good at it. Facts is what I deal with, no kooky conspiracy theories, UFOs or sightings of the Virgin. Everything in my life has always had a logical, rational explanation.

Until now.

When the stories first started coming out, I laughed, like everyone else. Yeah, right, of course an ordinary American kid has mastered flying. No aids, no contraptions, no tricks, he just flies. Never been done before and no logical explanation for it. He says he just figured it out. All over the TV, the internet, the tabloids and everyone says the same thing: it's real. Everyone says it cannot be, but it is. This kid is flying. I watch the TV, the videos, the whole shebang and I can't see what the trick is, and neither can anyone else. It doesn't make sense that there is no trick.

The kicker for me is that this isn't a kid out in India or someplace like that, not even California, Land of the Kooks, but here, in my own neighborhood in Maryland. My own backyard.

Well, I have a life. I am bugged by this stuff; quite frankly, when something makes no sense, it upsets me. I like an explanation. But I'm not one to obsess. I've probably seen the kid around, even before he became famous. His father hadn't been around for a few years, I'm told, the marriage broke up, but I think I may have said hello sometime. The mother's face is kind of familiar, one of the thousands you meet in a mall or a restaurant and nod at because you know you've seen them. For a while there are TV vans on that street and paparazzi, and when I go into Smitty's to buy ice cream, I see tabloids with Adam's face on the front cover, and flipping through channels I sometimes see him soaring through the air, or some bozo explaining what it must mean, but I don't pay that much attention. Lots of fires around, keeping me busy. The economy is in the crapper so people losing their homes and businesses figure the insurance company is stupider that they are, and they can walk away from the wreck of their lives with a few thousand dollars. I'm the hired gun who says no.

After a couple of months the neighborhood settles down, hardly any commotion in front of the house anymore. I read an article that says that if Adam Zajac teaches us to fly, we'll cut our dependence on oil, won't need cars and planes and trains, but it's all balderdash. Even if the kid is doing it, he's not teaching anyone, isn't explaining how he does it, other than "merge" and "commune" and no one's about to sell their car and fly unaided to Florida with those instructions.

But now there is no house. A hole in the ground is al, not even the foundations but the lawn is still as green as ever. In my work I examine physical evidence: brick, timber, furniture. The ground isn't even charred the way we understand charring. I'm working with the cops, of course, nobody is any wiser than anyone else and probably soon Homeland Security will come in and take over. The rumors are flying around anyway, even if Adam Zajac isn't. He's gone, poof, and so is his mom, in addition to the house. Martians took them, I heard, little green men in a UFO. And considering what we've already seen with our own eyes, the kid soaring, that's just as plausible as anything else. Maybe it's past the time for men of science. I can't trust my eyes. If a kid can fly, then maybe there are Martians abducting humans and incinerating houses in ways never experienced by science.

My brother sent me a Slovak folk tale by email. Our neighborhood flying miracle kid, he was of Slovak heritage. In this tale, a magical bird, Vtak Ohnivak, brings blessings and doom. He's a phoenix. He self-destructs, burns up, and then resurrects. So maybe Adam was a phoenix and that is why he could fly and somewhere in the world, or maybe on Mars, he's now resurrected. Makes as much sense as anything I've seen with my own eyes.

The other rumor flying around is that two armored cars and a limousine with government plates pulled up to the house in the middle of the night, that there were bangs and that our government used a secret substance to evaporate the house. Like drones. They have Adam now, and he'll teach them to fly and be a secret weapon.

I prefer the magical bird.

Friday

8

August
2014

At the
Bistro D'anglaise

by Rachel Ambrose

"Claire, this is your mother. Are we still doing that lunch date today? Call me," my mom's voice chirps at me far too early in the morning. It's a Friday, so usually I would be working, but Mrs. Hatfield has taken her yearly two-week vacation to Bora Bora, and the office is closed. In some ways it's nice: I don't have to slink around the office trying to get away with wearing as little as possible, and it's a good rest for me as well. But it does leave me with a lot of nothing to do, now that Isa has moved back in with me and Charlotte has moved out. And ever since last month when I broke up with Blake, more time on my hands has not been something I particularly like. It mostly leads to bouts of crying and, after, staring at the grubby gray ceiling in my room for long periods of time.

Hence the lunch date. I call Mom back and let her know that, yes, lunch is still happening, to which she replies, "Oh, good, I was hoping you'd say that, I'm going to be bringing someone along for you to meet, you'll love him."

"Excuse me," I say. "Him?" I had been under the impression that we were meeting at a cute little French bistro downtown for some much-needed rosé and chatter. Why does a man need to be involved for that? It seems like an intrusion.

"Trust me, darling," my mother says in a weird,

45

whispery tone, like she's keeping a secret from herself. "Dress up nicely and do something about your hair, it'll be fine."

I am armed with misgivings and do the precise opposite, slinging my hair back into a messy bun and putting on a paint-splattered dress that's a half-size too big for me. At the last minute, though, I add a few wooden bangles and a swipe of blue eyeshadow, just for appearance's sake.

Upon arrival to the restaurant, I take a look around and find Mom in a corner booth sitting across from a suave-looking olive-skinned man in a button down shirt. She catches my eye and says, "Claire, darling!" as I walk up to them. I wave back and she pats the seat next to her saying, "Claire, this is Frederico de Vera, he curates the art museum downtown, I thought it might be fun to bring him along." She takes a pull from her wine glass as a waiter fills mine and I nod in Frederico's general direction. Another art-world person? Didn't she know that I was just getting over Blake? I manage a "lovely to meet you," before diving into the menu.

"Your mother tells me that you dated Blake Easton for a while," Frederico says.

I almost choke on my wine before sputtering, "Yes, yes, for a couple of months, but it wasn't serious."

He surprises me by saying, "This may not be of much comfort, but I always thought his work sucked."

I find myself letting out a little chuckle, and I haven't laughed in so long that the sound almost shocks me. I look up and take another look at this guy – aquiline nose, slatey eyes, youngish, with an elegantly cultivated streak of gray in his hair. I raise an eyebrow. Maybe I don't have to hide in my rosé today after all.

Over lyonnaise salad and vichyssoise, Frederico stands up to the claims Mom made about me loving him. He lacks Blake's magnetism, but he's charming and funny and intelligent, three good points in his favor. I'm wondering, though, why Mom brought him along. Then he surprises me at the end of lunch, when we're all lingering over truffles and berry pavlova, by saying, "You know, I could really use a personal assistant at the gallery – you wouldn't be interested, would you?"

"Um," I reply, furrowing my brows and thinking of poor Mrs. Hatfield, but then I think of how stuffy the office can be and how boring my job actually is. Maybe this could be just the push that Blake was talking about, and I find myself nodding, a smile stretching across my face. "Yes, I am most certainly interested!"

"Fantastic," Frederico replies. "Come in on Monday for a test run. Livia, who's my personal assistant now but she's leaving to go to Paris, will train you. Keeping track of me isn't all that hard, but it does require a fine attention to detail."

I try not to gulp – at least if I'm awful at it, Monday was only an audition. I might even be good at it, who knows? "I'll be there at ten," I say, downing the last of my wine.

Where might one buy a fine attention to detail?

Saturday

9

August
2014

Callus

by Gill Hoffs

"What does your mother think you *do* for a living then?"

"Well –" I start to answer and he cuts in with "Ha! I suppose I should've asked you WHO do you do for a living!" and cackles out a laugh revealing dark fillings in his back teeth and thick yellow scum on the meat of his tongue. I imagine accepting a French kiss from this man – that curdy saliva being thrust into my mouth and the sour taste of it – and have to sip my tea quickly, despite its heat, to rinse the squirmy feeling away.

We are in a coffee shop near Deansgate, a decent one with the prices drawn in dusty white chalk on a giant blackboard behind the counter, the elegant angles of the 7s and 4s and the extra serifs on the 1s suggesting the European mainland was the baristas' original home. The whole place smells of fresh coffee and gingerbread and I regret hustling this noisy prick into a place I could've reserved for time off and rare rendezvous with real friends, if I'd known how nice it was inside.

"So d'you get to fuck anyone famous? Anyone I know? Hey – d'you fuck anyone from Creatlesby and Bartlette? You fuck my boss?" I can see him imagining some kind of powerplay with his unfortunate superior on Monday, his eyes narrowing with cunning, and swiftly shake my head, no. I *have* fucked his boss, imaginatively and enjoyably (for me, I mean – for my clients, enjoyment is a given), but the day I confess my client list is the day I leave my life, and by that I *don't* mean retirement, but for good.

This prick's my worst nightmare made real, with added halitosis and hair tufting out his nostrils, crusted with the yellow-white escapees of a million sniffs. I don't know how he knows about my life, or recognised me on the street – sure enough of himself to shout to me across the Saturday crowds hustling in and out of the Arndale Centre, "I know *you*! You're a callgirl!", obnoxious enough to demand an audience and explanation of my life – *my life* – with a broad Manc chatter of "How come you ended up shagging for money then? Watch too much 'Pretty Woman' as a kid, did you?" but here we are, in the emptiest café I could find, out of the bright heat of a northern summer's day, having a conversation I hate.

I am SO glad he's gay.

Previous iterations of this discussion or interrogation or lecture (depending on the dickhead burning with so much curiosity he just *has* to confront me, any or all of these descriptions could apply) have usually ended with a request / appeal / demand for a freebie. A quick lick / suck / fuck in the toilets or his car or a room nearby or even a full-on 'date' to a stuck-up sister's wedding. Not one of these awful encounters has ended in ejaculation, to my knowledge. Certainly not at my hands (or crotch or arse or tits or mouth). Thankfully this is unlikely to be an aspect of my career choice this droning tosspot will want to experience.

So far I have admitted nothing. My steaming Earl Grey (with milk – I know, I'm a disappointment to the human race) is my shield and I'm grateful for the café's air conditioning and how it allows me to sip and blow and cradle the mug in front of my face and hide while I gather my thoughts.

"Is all this sex the reason why your skin's so good? Do you even have to go to the gym to maintain that *fabulous* body? Or is it the sperm – you know, I read that cum facials are the key to staying young and gorgeous even into your forties – and champagne? I bet that's all you drink on your 'dates'," for goodness sake, he even wriggles his fingers in air quotes when saying 'dates', "it's alright for *some*."

And he sniffs so the clots of snot on his nose hair quiver and vibrate.

I wish my phone would ring or the fire alarm would meep or some fucker with an Uzi would run in and hold the baristas up. Just something, anything, to shut this nasty bastard up.

I slurp instead of sip my tea, savouring the bergamot, keen to make a noise of my own, and drown out some of his.

"What about your bits?"

Sweet jesus.

"Do you use some kind of salve to keep you supple down there? Stop the johns rubbing you the *wrong way*," and he sniggers at his attempt at a joke, "keep you limber for their timber?" And he's hooting and slapping the table now, the baristas looking over at this dickhead and his cringing companion.

If I 'drop' my drink in his lap, will he fuck off home?

Noooooo …

What if I dump it in mine? 'By accident.'

Maybe when it cools down a bit.

Yes, that's the plan.

I keep blowing on it.

"Whatcha going to do when your looks go? Soon your boobs'll sag, your looks'll go, and *then* what'll you do? Which of your sugar daddies and sad cases will put Cristal in your fridge and a cock in your hole then?"

He is really quite exquisitely offensive and I wonder if he's like this with his friends, if, indeed, he has any.

"What do you do for kicks? Are you vanilla on your days off?"

His voice is getting louder, grating in my ears, and one of the baristas, a woman with the dimples and generous smile of a young Tori Amos, keeps glancing over at our table.

"I mean, my careers advisor always told me if you do what you love you'll never work a day in your life." Fucksake, really? You're bringing out *that* old chestnut? "So I s'pose that's the real question, huh? Are you doing what you love instead of *who* you love? Huh? Huh?"

And he raises his eyebrows and nods at me like he's swallowed the collected works of Freud, Jung, Oprah, along with a box of fortune cookies, and is belching out words that should mean something in that order but really don't.

I blow my tea.

"Are you, like, callused?"

Now it's my turn to raise my eyebrows. Surely he doesn't mean …

"Like, vaginally?"

The barista is very still at the counter.

"You know what I'm getting at? Have you done it so much that you're, like, hard down there? Tough? Not that I'm an expert on ladyparts!" He's laughing again. "But that amount of sex'll surely get you calluses. Do you use moisturiser to keep you feeling right?"

Then the kicker.

"Do you have to pumice?"

And at this I cannot take his jibes and awful questions any more. The Earl Grey is out of my mug and onto his in one swift desperate action.

He squeals, I gasp, and the baristas applaud.

One shows him out, stuffing a bunch of paper napkins in his hand as they open the door, smirking at his discomfort. The Tori lookalike beckons me to the counter. As she makes me another drink, she offers me a brownie "On me" – oh, I wish! – and says, "My dad's been invited to my mum's wedding, and he needs a hot, classy date. How might he get a hold of you?"

And I smile at her, pinch a chunk off the brownie, and consider my day complete.

Sunday's Child

by Susan Tepper

Blisters on his heels. *Payless*. His feet are killing him. "You buy discount, those cheap sneakers that look good, you take a hit," he says getting out of the car.

He's back at the mall with the idea of returning the sneakers. Carrying them in the original box, receipt and all. *Payless* being at the cheap end of the mall where the kids shop. A cool spot. No expensive boutiques, no Bloomingdales, no snotty bitches toting mounds of high end shopping bags. Just Payless and a DQ and a GNC and some junk jeans stores. A *Life is Good* store that went out of business. Only the name remains on the glass. The kids like this end of the mall.

Pedersen enters through a side door, stopping to watch some real small kids dancing around on a musical mat. The more they dance the more music comes from that mat. Not a great sound but the little darlings just love it! The mothers, mostly fat and ugly, stand around talking to each other.

Tucking the sneaker box under his arm, he strolls toward the DQ. He'll have a dip cone. The chocolate in the big poster photo looks undernourished; like they didn't give it enough cocoa bean. "Is that dip chocolate dark?" he asks the DQ girl.

Behind the counter she has on heavy glasses and a stupid blue hat with red trim. The hat matching the rest of her uniform. She doesn't seem to understand the question 'cause she just stands there with her mouth dropped open.

"The dip cone," he repeats. "Do you dip into dark chocolate?"

The girl shrugs. "It's not white chocolate. If that's what you mean."

Damn! Pedersen is starting to sweat, feel nervous. Pulling on his shirt collar. "Dip me a large size vanilla cone, OK?"

Without answering, she moves like an ice cream robot. She takes a cone from the cone dispenser holding it under the soft serve spout. The vanilla comes out in a high swirl. At least she doesn't short change on the amount of ice cream. He's seen them give half that much and charge for a large serve.

Now he watches her do the fast upside down dip. At least she does it correctly. The new ones don't have the technique. It can be a mess. He pays, and she hands him one napkin.

While he eats his dip cone he wanders toward the mat kids. They're the same group: two blondish girls, a chubby girl about three years old, and a little dark boy of about five or six.

"Moosie," the mother calls out to the boy. At least what sounds like moosie to his ears. Pedersen can't make out half these foreign names. He decides it's a bad name for this boy who will turn out magnificent. He has the features and the compact, sturdy frame. Thick black hair. Moody eyes. A natural stud. You can't go around with a name like that, he's thinking.

He bites off some of the hardened chocolate, not as dark as he wanted. It tastes waxy. Then wiping his mouth with the napkin Pedersen strolls toward the mother. He stops a few feet away from the music mat. Catching her eye. He smiles and she smiles back. He catches some gold in her mouth. "Cute kid," he tells her.

The mother smiles wider.

"You ever thought about using him for modeling?"

The mother sort of brightens, waving fleshy braceleted arms around in an excited way. "You mean like the American Idol?"

"Well, yeah, sort of. Without the singing part."

He watches for a reaction. There is none. She's waiting for the payoff. Wants a big one. Pedersen sees the saliva forming at the corners of her mouth.

Paradiso Monday

by Jessica McHugh

He's surprised by how fast he found a gay bar. Venturing out of town doesn't usually stir his anxiety, but he's never made the journey to the city in high heels before. After parking in front of the Paradiso Club, Edward McKenzie tucks his crucifix under his dress and looks in the rearview mirror. The neon lights from the club sprinkle his face in pinks and oranges as he smears on a fresh coat of lipstick.

It suits you, sweetheart.

Eleanor pats his hand, her nails like withered roses compared to the brilliance of her grandson's. For his first night out, he's worn his boldest and most un-Edward outfit, dazzling with jewels and crisscrossing stripes of fuchsia and flame. The shift dress doesn't quite fit, but he's utilized a sweater to cover the loose spots wider hips would fill. Combing his fingers through his new wig, he frames his face with blond curls. Maybe he's not as beautiful as he could be, but when he smiles, he doesn't see Father Edward McKenzie, and that's all that matters now.

"This is it," he says to his reflection. Looking to his grandmother in the passenger seat, he purses his lips and exhales a quivering breath.

Do you want me to come with you?

He does, but he shakes his head. "I'll be fine on my own."

I've always known you would be.

She squeezes Edward's hand and disappears, but her warmth remains. He feels it even as he sets a tapered toe on the asphalt of the Paradiso, encouraging him. There aren't many other cars in the parking lot, but he didn't except many people to visit the club on a Monday night. Maybe if it goes well, he'll come back on a weekend.

He doesn't need Eleanor to remind him: one step at a time.

A Lady Gaga song pumps from the speakers inside the bar. For a moment he imagines it's Kay Starr instead, her silky song filling him with the confidence he feels at home. But the real rhythm soon takes hold and he sashays into the Paradiso.

"What can I get you, honey?"

He sits at the bar, blushing at the bartender's term of endearment.

"Ginger ale, please," he says, surprised by the natural femininity in his voice.

The bartender sets down the glass and pops a straw into the bubbling soda.

"On the house," he says with a wink. "This is your first time here, right? I think I'd remember a face that beautiful."

Edward bites his lip. He can't recall the last time someone complimented him on his appearance, if ever. He nods and watches the bubbles rising in his glass.

"What's your name, honey?"

Rather than looking the bartender in the eyes, Edward stares into the mirrored wall behind him. When he replies, "Eleanor," he really believes it for the first time.

"Pretty name," he says. "You live around here?"

Heat blooms in his cheeks. "There aren't places like this where I live."

The voice ringing from the corner is slurred but powerful. A drunken shuffle accompanies the stranger saying, "Then maybe you should come here more often."

Stinking of vodka, he oozes onto the bar stool next to Edward, wobbling. He finds the man familiar, but his slumped position and rumpled hair reminds Edward more of his mother, Betty, downing bottle after bottle at Shady Acres Nursing Home, than any man he knows. Leaning into Edward, the stranger's stench intensifies with a cackle.

"You know, this isn't a lady club."

The bartender shakes his head. "Cool it, Charlie. Everyone's welcome here."

The man laughs and pushes the hair out of his eyes. The name and another glance are all it takes for Edward to recognize Charlie Kitner, a parishioner from St. Peter's.

Fidgeting worsens his sweating palms. Edward hasn't spoken more than the few words necessary for communion to Mr. Kitner since the supposedly heterosexual married man confessed his attraction. He tilts his body away, sipping his soda in silence.

"You're a pretty thing. A little old for my taste, but that's not a dealbreaker."

Pointed in the opposite direction, Edward says, "If this isn't a lady club, why would you be interested in a lady?"

Charlie slaps the bar, punctuating his laughter. "You're a quick one. The truth is, I'm kinda like this place. Everyone's welcome," he says. "Let me buy you a proper drink."

"This drink is proper enough, thank you," Edward replies. "And I should be going anyway."

"You just got here."

Digging into his purse, Edward mumbles, "It was a trial run."

The bartender leans on the bar and says, "You don't have to go. If he's bothering you, I can kick him out, or send him back to his table. I've done it plenty before."

Sidling up, Charlie exhales boozy breath against Edward's ear. His dangling ruby earrings swing, and his neck prickles with goose bumps when the man purrs. "Yeah, make him send me back to the corner. I've been bad."

He instantly regrets getting angry over the man's brazen attitude, as well as giving him a clear view of his face when he snaps his head around. But most of all, he regrets the words he fires at the drunk. Charlie's eyes widen when Father McKenzie says, "It sounds like you have lots of sins to confess."

Edward watches the wheels turn in Charlie's foggy brain until he whispers, "Father McKenzie?"

Edward shakes his head as he places a five-dollar bill on the bar, and stands from his stool.

"Don't leave on my account. The night's just begun." Charlie's chin juts out as he smiles. "I won't tell anyone I saw you. Just like you won't tell anyone you saw me. Right?"

"Of course I won't."

He pats the barstool. "So sit down. Finish your drink. Let's pretend we're strangers," he says, looking Edward up and down. "It looks like you have a hell of a story to tell."

Edward's stomach turns. *A hell of a story* is right. Confidence drips down his face with his foundation. And though fear and doubt rise again, he doesn't let it show. When Charlie Kitner's hand slides up his arm, the knot in his stomach fires burning bile up his throat, but instead of doubling over, he shoots the man an icy glare and pulls away.

"Hey, you know how I feel about you. Whatever you are, whatever *this* is, it's okay. You don't have to be afraid of me," Charlie says.

Squaring his shoulders, Edward puffs out his padded chest and declares, "I'm not afraid."

"You're not going to give me that 'priests are celibate' crap, are you? We both know what you came here for."

"You're wrong."

Charlie rolls his eyes. "You frigid or something?"

"No, I'm just not interested."

Squinting, he huffs. "In sex?"

Edward's reply is more resolute than he'd thought possible, especially in Eleanor's voice.

"In you, Mr. Kitner."

While Charlie sits dumbstruck, Edward whips around, his golden hair bouncing as he strides to the door. Exiting the Paradiso, his body burns with pride, his cheeks aching from the strength of his smile. Inhaling the brisk August night, he's never felt so powerful. His calves burn as he strides to his car, the clacking from his high heels louder than the bass line pumping from the club. He won't be surprised if his strut cracks the pavement.

His joy survives the entire drive back to town. It isn't until he's home, removing his dress, that he realizes the possible danger he's welcomed by refusing Mr. Kitner. Sitting down on his bed, he rolls a rosary through his fingers and begs for Grandma Eleanor's advice.

The only Eleanor to visit him tonight will exist solely in his terrified reflection.

Opportunities / Escapes

by Shane Simmons

"New opportunities available. Location: SCOTLAND."

It's rare that anything on the notice board at work catches my eye (even if I had been told to pay more attention to the various signs that litter it). Someone must've had a cleanup of the usual out-of-date guff and there, pinned in the centre, is a mostly blank A4 sheet which I'm certain I've never spotted before.

"Enquire with your manager for further information."

The vagueness of these so-called 'opportunities' piques my interest, but for all I know it could be anything from a cleaner's position to the search for a new head honcho.

Scotland.

Mark was half-Scottish.

Perhaps that is what made me stop to take a look. I wish Sandra had never put him back there, in my consciousness. But who am I kidding? She didn't reinstall him. He'd never entirely left it in the first place.

Out of the corner of my eye I spot Malcolm, my line manager, approaching. He doesn't break his stride as he passes. "Bit silly, getting us lot to put that up there. But you know what they're like …"

§

I spend the rest of the morning thinking about *things*. About this job, where I am, where I'd rather be. What I should or even could be doing instead of being tied to a desk for most of the day. I check over scanned images for the archive one by one and I wonder where all my ambitions had disappeared to. And Mark once again crashes in on my thoughts.

I wonder if he ever thinks about me?

I catch myself grimacing in the faint reflection on my computer screen. I must be the last thing on his mind.

God, would he even remember me?

Just as I turn to exit the coffee shop, one hand grasping a brown paper bag containing a cheddar and ham toasted sandwich, the other wrapped around the obligatory midday coffee (always with one extra shot of espresso), I bump into Malcolm.

"Fancy joining me for lunch?" he asks.

It's a sun-drenched summer day and I really fancied taking up a bench over the road and watching the river. Instead, as he goes to order I spot a solitary empty table. The one by the swinging toilet door.

I don't mind Malc, he's quite a down-to-earth guy. Dull as dirty windows, but decent nonetheless. You could say he was part of the reason I got this job in the first place, what with his wife and him being good friends with Uncle John and Aunt Patricia.

But that also makes him one of the few who know the truth about my parents' demise. I can't help but feel that sometimes he looks at me in that sort of way. Head tilted slightly to the side, lips wincing under big cow eyes, reeking of unnecessary sympathy. I've never been one for sympathy. I didn't need it when they were here, and I certainly don't need it now they're gone.

Sitting down, he takes a bite and mumbles with his mouth full, "Best salmon and cream cheese bagels by the way!" He wipes the crumbs from his mouth and swallows. "Seen your John and Pat lately?"

"Not recently, but I keep up to date with them on the phone."

"We've not visited in a while. Really must head up their way one weekend. Nice neck of the woods."

Munching through our respective lunches, the surrounding hubbub doesn't make up for the slightly awkward silence.

"What's the deal with that new sign on the notice board?"

"The Scotland one? Goodness knows, I've not bothered looking any further into it. It's hardly as if anyone down here is going to ask about it."

Fat lot of good that was. I put down my sandwich and scratch the stubble on my chin. "So, no ideas what they're looking for then?"

With his coffee cup to his lips, one eyebrow raises higher than the other. "Why are you taking an interest in it?"

"Oh, just intrigued. You did tell me I should pay more attention to the notice board ..."

"I did, but I genuinely didn't expect a single soul to enquire about that." He rests his elbows on the table, leans across. "You're not thinking of leaving us, are you?"

Am I?

What *are* my intentions?

"I've long been meaning to have a little one-on-one chat with you," Malc continues. "You've been here well over a year now and we really haven't had much chance for any sort of appraisals. You know, snowed under with this never-ending backlog for the archive ... Do you know, there's talk of merging with English Heritage and taking on their archival inventory! We're nowhere near through our own yet!" Malc can make excuses as well as anyone trained in management can.

"You've slotted in well and really, we didn't expect much from yourself during your probationary period, but overall we have been impressed with your efficiency, as well as the quality of your work. Makes a change to have some young blood on the team." Seems he's adept with back-handed compliments too.

Back outside thin cloud cover masks the sun. I shake my head – "No thanks, I don't smoke" – to Malc's offer of a cigarette before he lights up as we stroll back to the offices. "You know, I lived in Aberdeen for a bit in my youth. Grey buildings, grey skies. It was always wet and miserable up there. Stay there long enough your skin starts to turn grey too!"

And back at my desk I think it over. Why *did* I ask about that notice? What's made me consider the remote possibility of leaving here? I've not got such a bad setup. What, if anything, is out there for me?

I notice a flashing light on my silenced phone. *No go tonite. Gf not going out now.* I sigh, relieved Callum's inconvenient girlfriend has forced him to cancel tonight's secret sordid session.

So, what *is* keeping me here?

Aunt Patricia and Uncle John. Two gravestones I can't bear to visit. A sister I couldn't care less about. A cramped flat and a job that pays my way but ticks too few of the boxes. Sandra. A fuck-buddy I know barely anything about. And memories.

Memories of a guy who's long gone.

And there's nothing. Nothing else at all.

I stroll over to the notice board. Hold my phone up and take a photo of that piece of paper. I upload it and stare it on the computer screen, wondering just what it's about. And if this is my opportunity to escape.

Just what I want to escape I'm still not sure of.

Cake

by Michelle Elvy

"Hey, haven't seen you around a while." Manny looks up from under the hood of an SUV, studies his friend as he enters the garage. The glare of the sun is behind Stevie, but Manny would know his walk anywhere.

"Yeah. Been kinda …"

"I know." It's always been this way with the two friends. They can finish each other's sentences or not say anything at all. They could spend all afternoon as boys, catching crabs down at the end of Spa Creek, and never say a word. In later years, they could drink a whole bucket of beer at the same dock, lying in the hot sun next to each other. Silent happy afternoons.

But now Stevie wishes Manny would let him talk, let him tell him everything about the last few weeks, how things with Ellie began so suddenly and now seem to have reached a momentum that won't stop. Stevie is scared of what he's feeling, of where this is heading, of whether his feelings for Ellie will keep him from going to Florida.

"You still goin' though, right?"

Manny puts down a screwdriver and walks to the folding chairs. Sits down and pulls out his smokes. He looks up at Stevie, his head cocked sideways, and grins. "You think I don't know what you been up to?"

Of course Manny knows. Of course he knows about her. Ellie. Stevie has not slept in weeks. He dreams of Ellie day and night. He's been dreaming of her for years, it turns out, but those were dreams he pushed away. Those are not the kinds of dreams you can let take form. Now, for the last month, he and Ellie have been … Have Been. Yes. Have. Been. That's as far as he can get because he can't name it but he knows whatever 'it' is is something that could be, yeah, love.

He walks over to Manny, sits on the folding chair beside him. Manny pours a coffee from the pot, burnt and stained but still with something passable in the bottom. He pours Stevie a cup, too. They drink coffee from Styrofoam for a few minutes, Manny smoking and leaning over, elbows on knees.

"See that piece of shit?" Manny nods toward the truck he's been working on.

Stevie shifts his gaze to the huge vehicle. Even from his vantage point from across the room, he can see it's almost new. Shiny. Midnight blue, almost black. Silver detailing.

"Owner's been in the shop every other day. Says we need to fix the motor. Fuel leak, he thinks. We been over it and over it. Nothing wrong."

"I don't get it. What are you gonna tell him?"

"That he bought a piece of shit car in the first place. You know what those cost? More than your college fund, school-boy. That's how much."

"And there's nothing wrong with it?"

"Nope. Fuel leak. Fucking idiot. Only thing wrong is that it gets ten shitty miles per gallon in the first place."

Stevie laughs at Manny's practical side. No room for flash in Manny's world. Manny's a hands-on kind of guy. A wild heart, sure, but a no-bullshit friend.

Stevie drinks more brown sludge. Wonders what he can tell Manny about Ellie. But Manny speaks first.

"So, Romeo."

Stevie drinks the dregs, studies the rim of his Styrofoam where his teeth have marked it ever so slightly.

67

"She goin' with you now?"

"Wha …? – No." Stevie hasn't put this into words since he and Ellie started being Stevie-and-Ellie, but he knows as soon as Manny asks that he will leave next month alone. That, whatever This is, it will end when he leaves Maryland, and that even if he and Ellie haven't spoken of it, they both know. So he clears his throat, says again, louder now, "No."

"I been wondering."

"Yeah. Me too. I can't even believe we've been …" He hasn't spoken to anyone about Ellie since she led him up her stairs for the first time last month. The only person he's spent any significant time with since then, besides his own family, has been her sister Sylvie. He has been at their house almost every day for a month.

"Her sister's kinda amazing," he says. And he realizes as he says it that this is not what Manny expects to hear.

"Her little sister? That little blonde kid?"

"Yeah. It's hard to describe. She's like Yoda in an even smaller package than Yoda. She's hilarious, and sweet. And she makes me feel …"

"Woah. Wait. You talking about Ellie or her sister?"

"Her sister. Sylvie. She's an amazing kid."

"So that's why you spend more time with Ellie, huh? You are re-living your *yout*!" Manny says it like a wise guy from Jersey.

"Na. It's hard to explain."

"I can play Jenga with you, man."

Stevie laughs and punches Manny's arm.

"But I can't suck your …"

"Hey." Stevie can't tell if Manny has stopped on his own or if he cut him off. Either way, he and Manny both shift in their seats, feeling uneasy.

"Seriously, though," says Manny. "You've had a thing for Ellie for … forever, I guess."

"Yeah, I guess so." Stevie grins to himself.

"You guys ever talk about …"

"No." This time Stevie knows he's cut Manny off. He doesn't want to hear the rest of that sentence. He doesn't want to hear Lucky's name. Lucky, who died in January when a car flipped and spared all of them, but not Lucky. Lucky, who was Ellie's boyfriend. Lucky, who was his and Manny's best friend. Lucky. Unlucky Lucky.

Just then Ellie walks through the door. Manny sees her first, stands up. She's wearing red shorts that swish a little, and a white tank top. Nothing special but enough to make him feel unclean, greasy. His dad's shop is always greasy, of course. But he instinctively looks at his fingernails as Ellie enters the cool of the garage.

"Hey you grease monkeys," Ellie says.

Manny hasn't talked to Ellie much all year. He saw her here and there during the school year but after graduation he didn't go looking for her. He'd seen Rick too, but he didn't want to talk to Rick. With Ellie, he always *wanted* to keep talking to her, but he was lost for words. What would he say? What *could* he say? It had been a shitty year for all of them, and nothing was going to change that. He and Stevie had kept close. But with Lucky gone, they'd lost some kind of glue that stuck them all together.

Stevie stands and points to the white box in Ellie's hands. "What's that?"

Ellie smiles. "Cake."

She pulls off the lid to reveal a small chocolate frosted cake with yellow icing sculpted around the edges. In the center is piped, in fancy scrolling, *Manny*.

"Happy birthday," says Ellie as she places the box on the table. When she pulls out a joint, Manny's smile grows wider. "For later," she says, and places it in his palm, folding his fingers around it. Manny looks down at Ellie's thin white fingers wrapped around his oily hand. She's cupped one of her hands under his now, the other on top.

She's holding his big ugly fist in her small hands, and she squeezes. She says again, "Happy birthday, Manny."

She releases his hand and steps back. The release washes over Manny and he knows now that all those things he didn't know how to say will never be said. That with this one small cake and those two hands wrapped around his, Ellie has found a way to fill in all that time, all those months of not knowing how to talk to each other. He knows they'll keep surviving the year that's impossible to survive. And he feels grateful – a catch in the back of his throat. Such kindness in those small white hands. Such sweetness.

Such friendship.

Manny turns to the coffee pot, his eyes hot. He shrugs his shoulders and sniffs hard, pours three small Styrofoam cups of coffee. He hands the cups to Stevie and Ellie. They push their cups into the air, into the space between them.

Manny looks at his two friends. Stevie, who is leaving. Ellie, who's come back.

He holds his cup of stale coffee high in the air. "To Lucky!"

Their Styrofoam cups smush together.

They eat cake.

Jerrod

by Len Kuntz

Outside of Akron, driving a beater car on Interstate 71, I pick up a hitchhiking dwarf.

Ordinarily I would never pick up a hitchhiker, but August in Ohio is a scorcher and I feel bad for the guy, not to mention (and this is me being judgmental, if not also bigoted) I don't see as how he could pose much of a threat.

He seems effervescent, amped up, both surprised and giddy that I've stopped. When he jumps in, sweat flicks from his forehead and splatters the dashboard so that it looks as if it's been crying.

"Thanks, pal," he says, holding out his hand for me to shake, which I do, trying not to cringe at how warm and moist it is. "Name's Jerrod."

There's still a bit of caution lingering in me, and I don't feel like telling him my name, so I lie and tell him I'm Clint, because I've been thinking of Clint Eastwood's *Dirty Harry* films for some reason.

"Where're you headed?" he asks.

"Don't know."

Jerrod laughs, a huge *I-just-fucked-your-wife-in-the-ass-last-night* laugh. "Come on, man."

"Okay, how about I'm on my way to Akron. You?"

"Akron," he says, disappointment scrunching his forehead. "Sure, Akron, that's my target as well."

So we're both drifters.

Much to my chagrin, Jerrod's a talker, blathering on about everything from Obama's daughters to the evolution of country music, how it's really just pop music without Auto Tune or lines about Hoe's and bling, and right at once I'm sorry I picked him up.

Then he starts with the questions: *What do I do?* ("Really? You lucky fucker, you actually have enough stashed away to just up and quit?") *Am I married?* ("You did the right thing, Clint, cutting the cord. A hag cheats once, she'll do it till she dries up.") *Why am I going to Akron?* ("Going to see your Sis, huh? You two must be close. I had a sister once, but she ran away at age *tennn*. Can you believe that? She hasn't resurfaced since.") *What kind of music do I like?* ("Bullshit, man. Nobody likes everything. Wait, so you like country music, I mean *real* country, Conway Twitty and Loretta Lynn?") *Who did I vote for in the last election? Have I ever seen a ghost? Do I wish I'd had children? Do I like spareribs? How many bodily scars have I got? Do....????*

It takes thirteen years or more until we finally see the road sign that says, **Welcome to Akron**. And underneath: **Home of LeBron James**.

"Shit," Jerrod says, suddenly anxious as a junkie, "Can you believe they're still loving on LeBron after he pulled that stunt and dumped the Cavs?"

I tell him I don't follow basketball.

"Fuck you don't."

I tell him I don't follow *any* sports.

He leans forward and turns to look at me, his face lit with astonishment. "Are you serious?"

"I am."

"And you're not gay?"

What if I was gay, I want to say. *What if I was gay, I* want to say, *and I pulled out a gun and put a bullet through your waxy forehead. What if I was gay*, I want to say, *so what? At least I can reach the dinner plates in the cabinets.*

72

But then it hits me that I've sunk to his level. Wait, that's bad, too. More bigotry on my part.

"Look," I say, "would it be all right if I let you off here?"

Jerrod's expression resembles a wife who's been told that her ass has grown fatter than her twin sister's. "At a truck stop?"

"We're in Akron."

"Can't you just take me where you're headed?"

"Where my sister lives is a residential area."

"So? Do I not look *residential* enough for you?" Jerrod holds his arms out, palms facing me, as if he's in a stick-up, and I notice in a flash, both how short his arms are, but also that he has huge hands, with fingers long enough to stretch across the entire radius of my throat.

"Hey," I say. "Easy, tiger."

Jerrod is panting now, breathing hard, his square jaw lowered, his eyes black bats swirling.

"No sweat," I say. "I can drop you there."

Jerrod blinks, blinks and blinks, and I wonder if I should ask if there's something wrong with him, but I don't want him to get more agitated.

"How far away are we?" he asks.

How should I know? I have no idea where I'm going, or where the residential sections are, yet I lie and say, "About twenty minutes."

"What's your sister's name?"

"Tawny." *Tawny. Why Tawny? Because it's the first thing that popped into my head and I once had a grade school friend whose sister was named Tawny.*

"She a good cook?" Jerrod asks.

Uh oh. Now he's expecting to be fed.

"Hey, Jerrod, this is all a surprise, you know, my stopping by. She might not even be home."

"That's not what I asked."

What did he ask? Oh, yeah. "Honestly, my sister's cooking sucks. You'd be better off eating dog food."

"Man, I'm starving."

"We can stop at McDonald's."

"Thing is, I'm broke, flat-busted."

"My treat."

"Really?"

"Yeah."

"Cool."

Jerrod smiles at me for the first time since I picked him, but I notice he's wringing his hands. I wonder if maybe the guy really is a junkie, though he doesn't look pale.

It's harder than you would think to find a McDonald's in such a big metropolis, but I do eventually. Jerrod doesn't want to do drive-thru, though. Inside, there's no line, which I'm grateful for. When Jerrod steps up to give his order, he takes a pistol out of his pocket and aims it at the stunned, teenage Hispanic and says, "Unload your till. *Now!*"

I try to remember where my own gun is, then realize it's back in the car.

"Hey, Jerrod," I say.

He tells me to shut my pie hole. To the clerk he shouts, "Hurry up! This is loaded," wiggling the snout of the pistol at the poor kid's nose.

When I turn to make a run for it, Jerrod swings his arm in my direction, aiming the gun at my crotch.

"Whoa!" I say.

"Clint, this was your idea," Jerrod says, enunciating too perfectly, clearly trying to set me up in the event this episode is somehow being taped.

"I had nothing to do with this."

"Now you're going to try and lie," Jerrod say, whipping the gun back toward the befuddled teller, then back at an obese couple who've just entered, telling them, "Get the fuck out! And find some fucking treadmills!"

The teenage clerk hands Jerrod a bag of bills in a McDonald's bag meant to hold a few Big Macs at most. Fives and Tens dangle over the lip of the sack.

"What about the change?" Jerrod says. "I want the change, too."

Once the till is completely emptied, we flee the place, Jerrod pushing my right ass cheek. "Hoof it! Cops'll be here soon."

When we get back in the vehicle, I'm so nervous I can barely slot the key in the engine.

"What's your problem?" Jerrod asks.

"My problem? You just held up a McDonald's!"

Jerrod waves the gun at me, and I notice how it smells like dirty underwear.

"You want I shoot you?"

I swallow. I think; it's been an interesting ride, my life these last few months. "Go ahead."

"Are you fucking nuts?"

"Shoot me if you have to, but I'm not driving."'

"I'll do it."

"Fine."

"Fine? Are you an idiot? You want to be dead?"

As if acting reflexively, I slam my palm into Jerrod's forehead and his skull smacks against the passenger side window. I stiff-arm him in the face again, and again. The gun plops on the floor mat. Jerrod starts whimpering.

"Why'd you do that?" he asks.

"Because you're the fucking idiot."

"But you don't understand."

"Get out."

"It's my girl. She needs an operation."

"Get out."

"She was born the wrong gender. She knew all along she was a she, I mean, he was a she."

"What?"

"Leslie wants to become my girl for real, but it's an expensive procedure."

When I pick up Jerrod's gun from the mat and aim it at him, he squirms.

"Get out now," I say.

"You ain't going to shoot me. I know that."

I fire a bullet into his leg. Jerrod squeals, shouting, "What the fuck, man?"

"I'll shoot again if you don't get out."

"All right. Fuckin' A, all right."

"And take your money."

"I will. Okay. Just don't shoot me again. Fuck, man, you actually shot me."

After Jerrod crawls out of the car, I peel away, tires screeching, rank smell of burnt rubber rising in the cab. I see a glimpse of Jerrod in the rearview, him squatting down near the kid's play area, obviously in pain. I floor the accelerator and get the car doing fifty and start thinking where I should dump the vehicle, wondering what Dirty Harry would do in a predicament like this.

Eighth Inning

by Michael Webb

I am standing outside, on the tiny balcony of my hotel room, feeling the breeze come in from Lake Michigan. Below me, taillights race away down Lake Shore Drive, Friday night lovers hurrying to a tryst, parents rushing home to see children off to bed, families headed off for the weekend. I watch them drive, standing there in a t-shirt and shorts, thinking about Don Henley's lyric that somebody's going to emergency, and somebody's going to jail.

There's nothing preventing me from getting dressed and going out. Every city, Chicago included, has steakhouses and bars and strip joints that will entertain a lonely man well into tomorrow. But I know better than to do that. The inflection point where that is worth both the effort to become presentable and the price to be paid the next day is different at 32 than it was at 22.

My phone, plugged into the wall on the bedside table, begins to warble. I glance at it, and then activate the FaceTime feature. My wife's face appears, her face slightly reddened, her hair loose, her eyes darting around the room. She probably just scrubbed off her makeup.

"Hi."

"Hello sweetheart. How are you? How are the kids?"

"I'm fine. Kids are good. Cuddle Bug misses you. I told her you're home Monday, and she said, 'how many day that?' I told her three, and she said, 'that too many day, momma'."

My heart pounds softly for a moment. Along with the massive paychecks comes equally large helpings of guilt.

"That's cute." She still alternates being wary upon my return with wanting so much attention crawling inside my skin would not be enough.

"Yeah," she says. Her eyes dart to the right, then center on me again. "Lucasita called an hour ago. You're not with Juan, are you?"

"No, hun. We all split apart when we got back to the hotel."

"If you see him, tell him to call his wife, OK?"

I try to imagine a situation where I would see Juan before the bus tomorrow morning. Yes, we play a game, but it's still a workplace. We don't hang out in each other's room and braid hair.

"Sure, hun."

"Marcy called and I bought a table for the art museum fundraiser."

I sigh, trying not to be audible. Another night of sitting around in uncomfortable clothes with people I don't like.

"I know, Mark," she says, picking up on my annoyance. "But Marcy is a good friend of mine. And she says I might get to be on the committee next year!"

I try to think of a reason why I should care about that. I paste on a smile. "That's great, hun. Did you watch?"

"The game? No, babe. I had to wrangle the kids, and then the phone hasn't stopped all night."

On some level, I am still 12 years old, trying to show off.

"How did it go?" she says, setting the phone flat to reach for something out of view. I can see the lights above her head, and a sliver of brown belly where her shirt gaps above her pants. She starts gargling with mouthwash.

"Not too bad," I say. "No runs charged. But we lost."

I only earned one out, and allowed 2 inherited runners to score, tying a game at 6 that we lost 9–7. In baseball logic, though, no runs were charged to me, so it was a fine day. I know she only really cares about outings that damage my stats, and thus my future earnings.

She leans over, her shirt and the shadow of one breast filling the screen as she spits out the mouthwash. I think about the easy, smooth way she moves, the way she seems put together, all curves and soft angles, by some higher, more intelligent power. I feel a stirring, my heart thrumming again at the impossible beauty of her, the way gravity pulls me to her, my heart as helpless to the laws as a comet.

"I have to go, hun. I promised Luca I would call her back. Talk to Juan, hun. OK? Love you!"

The picture disappears, and I say "I love you," to myself in an empty room.

I know I'm not going to talk to him, and she should know that too. Men aren't like that. It's one of the rules. And ballplayers certainly aren't.

I think about the throb I feel, the ache for her body, the need, her belly still taut and firm. The glow is fading now, my lust rapidly cooling in the air conditioning. I don't have to be alone tonight, if I don't want to. Everyone knows the bars where the groupies hang out. Or there are the escorts, or there are …

I stop myself. No there aren't, I think. You're not going to do that. You're not going to go chasing, trying to rut like an animal. You're going to turn on the TV, set your alarm, and go to sleep. I look around the room, remembering the nights she used to send me naked pictures of herself to get me through 4 nights in Cleveland, and I pick up the remote control. One of the PBS channels is showing something about Churchill. I turn the volume up, and open the minibar for some M&Ms.

Endangered Species

by James Claffey

The granite of the church sparks diamonds in the sunshine and the Bird takes a good look all round to make sure nobody's watching. He undoes his fly and streams his widdle into the outside holy water font. Quick as can be he slips his mickey into his pants and before he can zip up again a lorry slams on the brakes and he almost topples into the font with fright.

Back on the bicycle he pedals out the gravel driveway of the church and makes for Hogan's in Clara, hoping the fresh late-summer air will clear the fog from his head. Since the reading of the will he's spent more time out of the town than in it and his trips to Clara always bring him hope of seeing Melodie once more. He'd give his last euro to hear her play the tin whistle the way she had the night he first noticed her.

The fields he passes are busy with workers harvesting barley and wheat, the combine harvesters chewing up the crops in great mechanical bites. From the top of a nearby machine a farmer gives him a wide-arced wave. The Bird tips his hat, the handlebars wobbling a bit under his grip. The Clara Road is birdsong and clouds of raised dust, the scents of summer sultry and reminiscent of childhood when he'd take the road almost every day on his way to his favorite fishing spot. As a small boy he would spend weeks casting flies on the slow water, the trout and perch rising relentlessly to the bait. Lately, his fishing tackle gathers dust in the house not his own, and as he crests the first hill and the glint of river water catches his attention he feels a pang of not guilt, but deep sadness, knowing his summers are no longer plentiful and the gray hair continues to arrive.

A gutted cottage in an unkempt field reminds the Bird of his grandfather, a poor cottager who had been arrested by the police in the late months of 1920 and remanded on suspicion of being in the IRA. Only a letter from the local monsignor testifying to his character spared him a long spell behind bars. God, his father loved telling the story at Easter in the pub, always on the touch for a free pint or two. This, the Bird thinks, as he watches two swallows swoop into the shell of the cottage, might have been the very cottage his grandfather was arrested inside. His father said it had been somewhere on the Clara road, before the village proper.

The real criminals weren't the police who arrested his grandfather, he thought. No. The real bastards were the solicitors. The sting of the solicitor's words as he formally read the will and thus granted the deeds for the property to the nuns acted like a stone in the shoe for the Bird. He couldn't make it through even an hour without cursing his parents and their desire to add only further to the convent's wealth. If he could land that bloody Mother Superior with his long gaff, drag her by the bleeding throat onto dry land and gut the bitch …

"Come here to me now," he says, grabbing for the swallowtail that flits past his head, the bicycle teetering beneath him. He swipes and swipes again and misses, again and again. The flimsy creature is impossible to catch, and reminds him of Melodie and her own evaporation from his life. Strange, how one moment Life can be full of the wide acres of possibility, and the next as constricting a space as a coal cellar. He pushes down hard on the pedals and into the loneliness of the open road.

§

Hogan's is empty, the quiet deadly. The barman polishes glasses taken from the dishwasher, the only sound the squeak of the floorboards he disturbs with his motion. The Bird nods and orders a pint. The man fills the glass over half way and sits it impassive on the countertop. "It's like ripples in a pond," the Bird says, eyeing the settling liquid. The man simply nods, reaching for another wet glass to polish. After a minute he tops off the pint and sets it on a bar mat in front of the Bird. "Slainté," the Bird says, foaming his upper lip with the head of the drink. No answer.

"Will there be music this week?" he asks, running his eyes across the chalkboard near the door. He doesn't see the name of Melodie's group listed.

"Only what's there. Read it for yourself," the barman says, placing another glass on the counter, gleaming.

"Thanks for that. I see it all right. D'you see the group with the French girl at all?"

"French girl?"

"Melodie, her name is," the Bird replies, eager to engage the man in some conversation.

"Haven't seen hide nor hair of them this side of Easter," he says.

"Pity." The Bird sips the pint, watching the second hand on the clock stutter its way around the dial. All's fair in love and war, my arse, he thinks.

The pint drained, he plucks a note from his pocket and leaves it on the counter.

Outside, the threat of showers seems real enough as dark thunderclouds roll across the horizon. The Bird clips both trousers and pushes the bike along until he swings into the saddle and rolls towards home. Off in the distance a corncrake's plainsong catches his attention and he smiles to himself at the rare bird's song. He knows what it is to be running out of time, like the corncrake, a victim of modern life and changed farming techniques. The Bird and the corncrake are blood brothers, two of the wounded of this world. Like the corncrake, the Bird needs only the one mate, and like the poor bird in the distance, he is frantically seeking her out before the last few grains drop through the narrow neck of life's hourglass.

Peace and Utter Joy

by Gwendolyn Joyce Mintz

A 'Back-to-School' event at the restaurant / bar where they work keep Aaron and Mora from making the meeting. It's Sunday besides. Diane has suggested that she and Phil take in a movie.

"Not in the mood for death and drinking," she tells him.

As they stand in line for tickets, Diane slips her left arm around Phil's right one.

It is a friendly gesture, he knows. Still, he says, "I wonder if guys are wondering how I scored you."

Diane leans over and kisses him on the cheek. "Wonder what they're thinking now."

Phil finds no malice in her face. "Did you do that because you pity me?"

Diane shakes her head. "Nope. Got a new motto: I'm gonna die, no need to lie."

"Kind of corny."

"Maybe. But if I felt pity for you, I would've kissed you on the lips."

Phil rears his head back, groans. Looking again at her, head tilted to the side, he pleads in a playful manner, "Please feel pity for me."

Diane giggles. Moves closer, leans against his arm.

Phil is buoyed by her sweetness and the moment swells around him. A moment he never thought to have: one of peace and utter joy, a beautiful woman beside him.

Wounds

by Stephen V. Ramey

"Hey, Mac, wake it up." Something prods my side. A tinted window blunts the light, but the sun is still hot on my face. I turn away from it.

"Come on, Mac, I don't got all day." Another poke.

A bus driver leans over me from the aisle, light blue shirt, narrow tie, nametag I can't read. I rub my eyes and sit straight. Usually I'm a light sleeper, but lately the ache in my hip has been keeping me from getting any real rest. I'm constantly fatigued.

"Yinz can't sleep here," the driver says. He points to a *No Loitering* sign amid the glowing ads along the bus' angled ceiling. I smell his cologne, pungent like Old Spice only fruity.

"I bought a ticket." I wave my pass book. One of the tricks Dave taught me was to buy a bus pass book and ride around all day. It's safe and more comfortable than a concrete floor.

The driver shrugs. "Look, Mac, I don't mind hauling yinz around – ain't like we don't have empty seats – but don't get on this bus again 'til you wash off some of that stink. I get complaints." The four or five passengers are looking at us. It makes me itchy.

"Don't make me call the cops, Mac."

"Okay, sure," I say. "I'll get off."

The driver returns to the front. I grab my backpack from

under the seat and stand. My knee nearly crumples. I've had some issues of late. All this walking is wearing me down.

The side door accordions. I spill through it to a sidewalk on the edge of downtown. A flyer taped to a metal light pole catches my eye. It's me, shaved, round-faced, almost smiling. *Have You Seen This Man?* There's more, but I don't bother to read it. Fat chance anyone's going to recognize me from that photo. My beard is like a bird's nest now, and my cheeks have lost their plump. I still wear glasses, but they're taped, the frame bent across my nose.

I shamble toward the Riverplex. A woman with a little girl crosses the street to avoid me. I don't take offense, in fact what I feel is relief. No need to be on my best behavior for ten or twenty strides. And my hip really aches now. The pain has spread into my lower back. I need to find a space to bed down even though it's barely noon.

East Washington is busy with traffic. Hot smells, metal smells, a hint of blue exhaust.

"Stephen?" The voice comes from several yards behind me, husky and female. It sounds like Rose.

I step into the crosswalk. An SUV rolls to a stop a foot from my shoulder. Chrome winks. I continue across the street.

"Stephen."

I move across the Riverplex as fast as my hip allows. Only when I turn behind The Confluence do I sneak a look back.

There's no one there. I continue around the corner into the wedge between buildings where they keep the dumpster. The scent of rotting vegetables greets me. Shade cools my head. I relax despite the smell. I probably smell worse.

I pull the tarp from my backpack. This is as safe a place to bed down as any on short notice. The dumpster will block me from view if someone walks past.

"'Sup," a man says. He's tall and slightly bow-legged, with a leathery face that recalls the Marlboro Man. He must've followed me.

He comes closer. "This your digs?"

"Public space," I say. "No one owns it."

The stranger snorts. "I got snipe, you want …" He flashes a baggy holding partially smoked cigarettes.

"Don't smoke," I say.

"Square's fine by me," he says. "I'm new. Know any good squats?" His eyes roam the alley, the dumpster. He chuckles. "Guess not, huh? How long you been on the street?"

"Long enough," I say. I spread the tarpaulin on the ground, keeping one eye on the stranger.

He strolls casually to the opposite wall. "Mind if I sack here?"

"Free country," I say. I don't mean it, but what can I do? He's bigger than me, meaner than me. I guess I could abandon the alley, but that would only reveal my fear. Plus Rose could be snooping around out there.

He settles down against the wall. His eyes close. I wait until his breathing is slow and steady. Then I lay down, using the backpack as a pillow, and close my eyes too.

Sunshine. Anne, laughing, runs to me through a field of grass. Her eyes shine with the same chlorophyll. I brace to catch her.

Something presses down. Breath squeezes out. I try to roll. An arm pulls around my throat.

"Where do you keep your stash?" Of course it's the stranger. I squirm, but he knows his leverage like a wrestler.

"Give it up," he says. "I know you got something." His forearm compresses my neck. A pen knife glints.

"Sock," I choke.

He rolls off, keeping the knife in view. Wheezing, I pull up my pant leg, roll down the sock, and peel two twenties from my ankle.

He licks his lips. I toss the bills. He scrabbles to get them before the breeze. I think of running, but he's between me and the exit. *Stupid wind.*

He tucks the cash into his pants. "That all you got?"

"Yeah." I spread my hands.

"Why don't I believe you?" He motions with the knife. I climb to my feet, back pressed to the dumpster.

"Empty your pockets," he says.

I turn out the left and let coins spill. He doesn't chase, doesn't bat an eye.

"And the other?"

I sigh and pull the wallet free.

He reaches. "Thought I saw a bulge."

I make a break. Pain flashes. My hip locks. The stranger tackles me before I reach the alley mouth. Breath flushes from my lungs. My palm stings. Asphalt bakes my cheek.

"You dumb fucker," he says. His fist pushes against me. I feel a new pain beneath my ribs, sharper, deeper.

He rolls off. I sprawl forward, but my side hurts so hard I see stars. My whole body goes limp. I reach for my gut, and blood coats my fingers. *Stabbed.* A sense of wonder comes over me. For an instant I revel in the thought of life leaking out, but that makes no sense. It's only a pen knife.

The stranger stands and harvests my wallet. "Three bucks? You have got to be kidding me, Einstein." He takes a bankcard from its slot and holds it to the light.

"Fuck," he says, and tosses the card down. "You ain't going nowhere." He glances at the plastic insert. "This your girl?"

I nod. Pain throbs through me.

"Alive?" he says.

"No," I say. Tears cloud my eyes. The thought of this man harassing Anne, touching her, makes me groan.

"Sorry for your loss," the stranger says. He tosses the wallet into the dumpster and strolls away as if nothing has happened.

How can anyone do that? How can you stab a man and walk away? And then I think, *How can I just walk away from Anne?* Maybe I deserve this, maybe I'm meant to bleed out in an alley with no one the wiser.

The sun creeps overhead. I feel its heat, yet I'm cold inside.

A man appears from the head of the alley. He walks toward me, using a cane. *Step-click-step.*

Is this God? The other guy?

"You're hurt." His voice is soft. He kneels down and feels my pulse. "I'm going for help."

"No." I push onto my arms. The wound tears and pinches as if the knife has slid into me again. My elbows collapse. I sink down onto my belly.

"You need a doctor."

"I'll be okay." *No doctors, I'm done with doctors.*

"I can't just leave you here," the man says.

"Please," I say. "It's only a flesh wound." I try to chuckle. It hurts.

"My name is Frank," the man says. He grasps my shoulders and helps me sit.

"St – Jimmy." I picture Jimmy's broad smile, hear his laugh. He would stick his fingers into my wound if he caught me posing as him. *How's that for funny, Stephen?* He doesn't like people stealing his material.

"Is there someone I can call?" Frank says.

"No. It's ... complicated. Just help me up, I'll be fine."

He shakes his head, eyes fixed on my bloody shirt. "If you insist on being stubborn, at least let me bind your wound. I was a medic once. I'll bandage you up, and then you can decide where we go from there."

He extends his hand, and I grasp it between my own, wincing at the sight of dried and half-dried blood on my fingers. He does not pull away, and a surge of gratitude flows. Frank is the opposite of the bus driver. They cancel each other out.

He leans back, and I pull myself to my feet. I wonder what the ducks on the river must think as we exit the alley, me leaning heavily on Frank, Frank leaning on his cane. I think of my blood smearing his suit jacket, my grime embedding in the fabric. It disgusts me.

"Sorry," I mutter.

"It's nothing," Frank says. "I have other suits."

Unravelling

by Gay Degani

Sybil is naked in her bed, sleeping off Margaritas, her windows open because of the heat, the air as dry as ash, wildfires in the nearby hills sucking up oxygen. The shouts are part of her dream – a dream in which she scrambles down the corridor of a speeding train, children and old men blocking her way. She leaps over dogs, shoves conductors into seats, then finds herself clinging onto a window ledge outside the passenger car, sand and wind blasting, mountains hurtling, and all the while, there is yelling, yelling, and now barking …

She wakes up. The barking doesn't stop. Neither does the yelling, the unfamiliar voices quickly familiar. Ian Shane from next door and – is that Gus' son, Mars? Of course it is. Ever since Ian's mother and Mars jumped into bed together, the tension between lover and son has crackled every time they meet. Sybil grabs her robe from the floor and glancing at the clock – 1:00 AM – she scurries into her living room to peek from behind the curtain.

Light blazes in Ian's bungalow, his windows flung up because of the heat, while Gracie barks in Gus' open doorway as the old man stumbles past her onto his porch. Then, as Sybil watches, Gus tumbles down the steps, landing on his side on the sidewalk. She's out the door, hurrying to him, shouting "Mars! Ian!" as she goes.

Reaching the old man, she stoops down. He groans, "My hip, my hip." Gracie whines and sniffs.

"Is it broken?" Sybil glances over his crumpled body, hollers, "Mars, come help!" The courtyard is silent, empty. The eyes of a coyote glint from the middle of The Old Road. No one is rushing out to help.

"I'm calling an ambulance," she says to Gus. "Do not move."

She straightens – her bones creaking – and hurries up Ian's steps, pounds on his door, opens it.

Ian is rolled into a ball on the floor, arms and hands bloodied, the glass coffee table shattered. Mars stands over him, fists clenched. She shivers in spite of the hot night air, keeps her voice low, but firm. "Mars, your father's fallen down. Go outside and see to him while I call an ambulance."

He pivots toward her, his face bewildered, and mumbles. "He's okay. I only hit him once. Not that hard."

"Go take care of your father. Now." She pushes him toward the door and he goes, slowly, reluctantly.

Ian, wearing only boxers, is unfolding on the floor. She leans over him. "Are you cut? How bad?"

He extends his arms, both dotted with small cuts and a thin slash along the side of his shoulder about two inches long. Bleeding, but not gushing.

"Okay," Sybil says. "Stay still. Let me call an ambulance and then we'll see how bad it is. Where's your phone?"

"In the bedroom."

Sybil tightens the raincoat she grabbed before driving Mars to the hospital. In the emergency waiting room, Mars slumps over his knees in the chair opposite her, his face concealed in his hands. He's been this way for the better part of an hour. Gus and Ian are beyond the swinging doors and Ian's mother is on her way.

"They'll be all right," Sybil tries to reassure him. Ian will, she knows, because his wounds are superficial. She doesn't know about Gus. Broken hips often lead to decline in the elderly, she thinks, forgetting that Gus isn't all that much older than she is.

The door to the waiting room whooshes open and in stumbles a nervous, disheveled woman, and at first, Sybil doesn't recognize her, but then recognizes the designer handbag Ian said he spent $1200 dollars to give his mother, money he doesn't seem to have and ridiculous since she pays his rent. But it *is* Rita Shane hesitating in the doorway, despite the messy hair, the sloppy sweatpants, the tattered t-shirt, all polish and brisk professionalism gone.

"Mrs. Shane." Arranging a reassuring look on her face, Sybil leaps up to greet the real estate agent, but the woman doesn't see her as she marches toward Mars and throws herself at him, falling against him, pummeling with her arms, growling obscenities. A male nurse rushes forward and grabs Rita Shane by the shoulders, trying to pull her off Mars while a voice calls for help over the intercom. Sybil stands frozen, her mouth forming an '0'.

Mars doesn't move. Lets her beat down on him, even as the nurse and security guard pull Rita Shane off him. The woman holds up her hands to show she's done and backs three or four steps away.

Sybil looks at the guard, hoping he takes the woman to some security office to cool down. But after the two of them confer in whispers, he puts a hand on Rita Shane's shoulder and nods.

Rita Shane glances past Sybil as if she were no more than a hat rack, and wags a finger at Mars, but when he doesn't look up – he's studying the carpet squares at his feet – the woman heads through the swinging doors. *To see her precious son* is the thought that flashes through Sybil's mind.

The nurse crouches down beside Mars who shakes his head and shifts toward the wall.

The nurse returns to the emergency room while the security guard heads down a corridor toward the lobby and only then does Sybil find her feet and return to her chair and sit down.

"Mars?" she says gently. He doesn't answer, but lifts himself from his chair and moves trance-like across the waiting room and through the door into the night.

She picks up her purse and puts it on her lap. She folds the handle over itself, then lets it go. She rummages for her phone and wraps her fingers tightly around it. She has no one to call. She drops it back into the purse and puts the purse back on the floor. Stretches her legs.

These are the times she thinks about Jamie. If Jamie were here, the two of them could form some kind of shield around Mars. They could stand guard and protect him from – who? Sybil pulls her feet in and tucks them under the chair. Himself? Of course. A middle-aged man who needs someone to protect him. It certainly wouldn't be Gus. She sighs, picks at her peeling nail polish. Men are more fragile than people think. Tougher than women on the outside, but inside. Why else do they die first?

These are the things she would explain to Jamie. About men. Some men. Most men. And about women like Rita Shane. How they tumble through life blinded to the faintest outlines of love and kindness, self-worth and contentment. And what good is having earned wisdom if there's no one to listen? Jamie had been a tenant too, but they'd become friends, the young mother with two little darlings and an irresponsible husband. The windstorm that blew through the Old Road at the first of the year toppled more than just trees. Then her mind wanders to the other missing woman, the one who lives on the other side of the Trencher mansion. Charmaine. Like with Jamie, no one knows what happened to her. Sybil shivers. Reminds herself that Jamie took her car, her kids, she has an aunt in Oregon.

A doctor, Sybil can tell by his confident stride, comes in from the emergency room and says to Sybil, "Are you Mrs. German?"

"No, I'm not." She stands up, holds out her hand. "I'm Gus' landlady and a friend."

"What happened to his son?"

"Oh. He – he went out for some air. Is Gus going to be alright? Did he break his hip?"

"I really need to talk to a member of the family."

"Okay, I'll see if I can find him, but Gus is okay, isn't he?"

The doctor nods, his mouth an impatient frown. "Yes, yes. Lucky for him, it's just a bad bruise, but have his son talk to the nurse when he shows up, will you please?" He turns and quickly disappears behind the double doors.

Exhaustion takes Sybil by surprise as she sinks back into her chair, her only thought, *If Jamie were here, I wouldn't be all alone.*

I would have the strength to go out and find Mars German and drag him back.

I will do that.

In a minute.

She breathes in and out.

In and out.

Musical Moments

by Sally-Anne Macomber

To: Milton Flaxmill, Red Cow Publishing
From: Trudy Polaris
Date: August 20, 2014 8:03 a.m.
Re: Creative Tension

Phew! I am just back from rehearsal and am brimful of energy so I thought I would write to you again Milton. *Fortune favours the fortunate* (is that the saying?) so I have decided to burn the Tyrolean voodoo dolls and make my own fortune.

I have long been fascinated by the works of the absurdist Eugène Ionesco. (You know, the Romanian playwright who wrote mostly in French? I met him once, on a tour of Parisian nursing homes – oh, it's a long story, Milton, but I will spare you the dramatic details because I have such *extraordinary* good news.) My favourite work of his has always been *Rhinocéros*, ever since I first read it as an eight year-old on an accelerated learning programme. Perhaps you know the play?

Well, I have been feeling especially musical since we arrived here in the Tyrol, the air is so fresh and creamy, and I had the strangest dream a little over a month ago – strange I did not mention it in my last email to you – but in the dream, I was touring the local zoo and was struck by a singing rhinoceros. This image was so strong it stayed with me after I woke up, and then while I was eating my morning Alpine muesli I just started singing gibberish.

"What are you doing? Singing Romanian?" my husband said to me across the table, his mouth half-full of half-chewed Old Viennese imperial omelette. (His manners have deteriorated the higher we go in altitude, it's crazy! And what makes the omelette so Old Viennese imperial? Strawberries!)

But it was like an epiphany. *Rhinocéros* the musical! (Except I called it *Rhinocérosi*) I bribed old Klaus next-door to milk the goats and wrote the musical in a day and an evening, 10 songs and the music and the script. (Though don't they call the script *the book*, in musical theatre circles? Milton, I have *so much* to learn!)

My husband fed me mushrooms and schnitzel and Edelweiss Schnapps when I called out for them. I was like Beethoven possessed, but at a higher altitude and possibly with a more subtle (or *subtler*?) tuning fork.

And luckily I've met a few musical people up here in the Tyrol, mainly through my ill-advised attempt at *dirndl* catwalk modelling (those laces on the bodice do *nothing* for an uneven cleavage) and within a few days we had the show cast and a rehearsal schedule mapped out … and then came the bombshell. Some well-meaning schmuck on the next mountain over was doing exactly the same! except he was mounting the 1990 musical version of *Rhinocéros*, called *Born Again* (What a stupid title! No wonder it completely passed me by!) and first staged at the Chichester Festival. (In fact, I may have seen it then: I was in Chichester in late 1989 and stayed a little longer than intended due to an extended airline pilots' strike. Which may explain the strange dream I had about the singing rhinoceros just over a month ago, which I think I forgot to tell you about in my last email.)

So it was back to the drawing board. Or rather, the harmonica. (The rooms are a little smaller than you might think up here in our Tyrolean hideaway, and even a keyboard is impossible to fit into the cramped music room, once you squeeze past the kettle drums aka *timpani*.) So I bribed Klaus to come back again to milk the goats (I told him he was going to be famous one day for knowing someone famous) and rewrote most of the songs in another all-day-and-night session, throwing out only one of them and adding two more because I was on a musical roll. I have based this new work on Ionesco's *Les Chaises* (or *The Chairs*), set it in Andalusia rather than the original Paris and called it *!Sillas¡ !Sillas¡ !Sillas¡* (which is *Chairs! Chairs! Chairs!* in español).

Which brings me to the point of my email: the dedication in *Nuclear Fission in The Pyrénées*. I know I originally dedicated it to my son i.e. *For my son*. Luckily, I only have one son, because changing the dedication would then prove even more difficult.

Given the influence I am now feeling since I immersed myself in Ionesco specifically and the Theatre of the Absurd more generally, I would really like to rewrite the last third of the book in a more absurdist fashion. But I am going to spare you that particular heart attack and say that instead, I would simply like to change the dedicatee to Eugène Ionesco, and I would like the new dedication to read,

ytidrusba etelpmoc ni
retsaM eht rof
ocsenol enèguE

Don't worry about the possible psychological impact this betrayal of a thirty-year promise will have on my son. I will square it with him with some ice cream.

The only thing that can top the genuine creative excitement I am experiencing at the moment, is an email from you.

Yours, and passing no value judgements,

Trudi Polaris

To: Leonard Strauss Jr., Red Cow Publishing
From: Trudy Polaris
Date: August 20, 2014 1:27 p.m.
Re: Absurdities

Schöne Grüße im Sommer, Herr Strauss!

I wrote an email to Milton Flaxmill earlier this morning and of course, have received no reply as yet. Though I remain ever-hopeful. Of course, I have also not heard from you since my email *to you* dated 20th July either but that was my first email to you and so, of course, you have a little catching up to do re neglecting your email replies to me.

Are you reading this as diligently as you can?

The reason I sent Milton an email is because I advised him I want to change the dedication of *Nuclear Fission in The Pyrénées* (originally *Nuclear Fission in the Pyrénées* and soon to be, if you did as I asked in my last email, *Nuclear Fission in The Himalayas*) and I want the new dedicatee to be Eugène Ionesco, whom I know is Milton Flaxmill's favourite playwright. I made up some crazy story about writing and rehearsing a musical version of *Rhinocéros* which is just the silliest thing to contemplate but there you go: I'm a career writer in for the long haul.

And I think the new dedication will get me in good with Milton and speed this editing process up.

(Don't ask me who I had to do to find out he's a fan of Ionesco: just know that it involved a lot of grinding. The bad thing is though, I had to change my whole story because some wacko on the next mountain over came up with the very same story to impress *his* publisher. Jeez, this writing / editing / publishing world is a small place!)

So where do I come in, you ask? Or rather, where do you come in, I say.

Well, *Nuclear Fission in the / The Pyrénées / Himalayas* was originally dedicated to my son Boy. (Short for Boysenberry, a now rather embarrassing I-was-a-hippy-for-18-months reference to the bush under which he was conceived, though he prefers people to think *Boy* is short for *Boyd*, so please, when you meet him, don't tell him I told you his real name is not *Boyd* but *Boysenberry*. He can be a little temperamental about it.)

So I had to come up with some pretty amazing thing to sway him from suing me for breach of promise, now that the dedication is going to Eugène Ionesco, so I told him you had promised him an internship at *Red Cow Publishing*.

Boy is on an athletics tour of the US at the moment and hits Boston tomorrow. He has blue hair and is in a wheelchair. He will be easy to spot because he is the über-talented shotputter.

His other particular skill is with languages, which you as the Dialect Editor / Janitor will probably find useful. He does not take up a lot of room and loves Boston accents.

(You will probably find an appropriate intern-sized desk for him in the basement, which you as janitor would have the key for.)

I see your sister Frau Erdbeeren quite often in the street. I would like to thank her for giving me your email address but usually she is in the distance so I just see the back of her disappearing head.

Grüß Gott,

Frau Trudi Polarissen

Purple Elephants

by Mandy Nicol

"Read it again and tell me what you think," Mum says, bouncing around in her chair and waving the letter at me. She's moving about so much that Seph jumps off her lap and trots over to the heater to edge Peregrine out of the warmest spot in the house. I snatch the piece of paper from Mum with one hand and use the other to cram the last piece of toast and vegemite in my mouth. This stifles any swearing at the breakfast table. I scan the page.

> *Dear Mum,*
> *Sorry I've been a little lax with my letter writing these past months, but you can imagine how hectic my life is over here in the 'Big Apple'.*
> *Anyway that's all about to change. I have some great news ... *** drumroll *** ... I've decided to come back to Australia!*
> *I've had an idea banging around in my head for ages and it's getting more and more insistent. I know it's time to act now. It will be a life changer, that's for sure, and it will involve big family decisions but it will benefit us all, I'm sure of it.*
> *I'll go through everything with you when I get home, which will be some time before*

Christmas. When I have the exact date sorted
I'll let you know so that Nadia can pick me
up from the airport.
    All my love,
    Anthony

I toss the letter on the table. "I have no idea what he's talking about. He doesn't actually say anything except he's coming to Australia."

Bloody prick, he wants to sell the farm.

I jump to my feet, nearly knocking my chair over backwards. "You'll just have to wait till he gets here to find out," I say.

Mum folds the letter and feeds it into its envelope. "We'll all have to wait, you mean. He says it involves all of us. At first I thought he wanted me to sell the farm, but now I'm not so sure." She tucks the envelope into her cardigan pocket. "It's not as if he needs the money, and where would you and I live? Plus there's old Jack's lease on the land, he can't just up and move his crops and cows at the drop of a hat."

No he can't, can he? I hadn't thought of that.

I smile.

Mum looks over at the dogs, clicks her fingers and pats her thigh. Seph opens one eye but otherwise takes no notice. Peregrine waddles over. I think I'm feeding him too much. "Of course I could set it all in motion," Mum adds, turning back to me. "But it would be months before anything could happen."

I stop smiling and gather up the dishes. "You wouldn't really consider selling the farm, would you?"

"Of course I would, if it was for the best."

I'm not as careful as usual with her butterfly teacup and she winces when it clinks against the plates.

"Still," she says, "Anthony could have anything up his sleeve, you know what he's like." She stares out the window, through the driving rain, probably remembering a cherub-faced boy playing with his toy tractor in the yard.

I remember that boy throwing rocks at me.

"You're right, Nadia, we'll just have to wait till he gets here to find out what his plans are. In the meantime we'd better get his room ready. For a start you could make some nice new curtains, he's a bit old for purple elephants."

The dishes rattle and clunk as I thump them back down on the table. "Hang on a minute, he's not getting his old room back, that's my sewing room. We don't even know how long he'll be here."

"Of course he can have his old room back, and there's no need for you to look at me like that. I've told the three of you that your rooms will always be here whenever you want to come home." Mum shakes her head at me as if I'm a naughty toddler.

I feel like a naughty toddler. I want to stamp my feet and start squealing. But I don't. I just say, "You never told me that, because *I've* never left."

Friday

22

August
2014

Ned Makes Friends

by Margaret Bingel

Nadia slows to a stop. The smells outside make her nose wiggle, and she can smell the stink of other dogs nearby. She squats down next to a bush and urinates. An unsuspecting squirrel on the ground is almost hit by the hot stream of piss, and it runs away, chittering insults.

Ned tugs on her leash one more time to get her moving, her legs sluggish from the heat. He doesn't want Nadia to get too fat at home, and besides, the walks in the park are really great exercise for his legs and lungs. Ned moves a lot more confidently now, hardly a limp left in his legs while he promenades down the concrete walk of the city park, the afternoon haze making everyone lazy and dull. Even so, the park is full of people lying about, or playing games on the grass.

Once Ned was comfortable with Nadia, he looked up places for the two of them to go so they can both get some exercise. At first he was ok with just sitting at home, surfing the Internet, but Nadia demanded more than just walks up and down his neighborhood. The vet told him that she was only 3 and needed more play time, preferably outside. So, Ned found a dog park within reasonable walking distance for both of them, and he makes it a point to bring her out every day.

Ned sits down on a bench to rest. The humidity is thick enough to coat the back of your throat with thirst, and

105

luckily, Ned had the wit to bring water for the two of them. He forgot about it last time, and Nadia was so tired he had to carry her home. Now, if it's too hot out, Nadia sits crossways through the doorway, not budging until she hears the faucet run.

Ned pulls a bowl out of his rucksack and pours water from a plastic bottle into it, then pushes it towards Nadia. While she laps up the water, he pulls out an apple and bites into it, careful not to let the juices run down his chin. There is a comfortable silence between them, the man and his dog, and with it, Ned feels time move slowly, each second like a drop of molasses dripping out of a bottle. So much better than the break-neck speed towards death he was feeling at the beginning of the year.

"So much better than in a long time," Ned muses aloud.

Once Nadia is done drinking, Ned packs the bowl and the bottle in the rucksack and holding her leash, walks over to the dog park. He enters the fenced-in area where all the other dogs roam and unclipping her leash, watches her run wild with the rest of her kind, free and uncaring. Sure, she's just a dog, Ned thinks, but she has a much better sense of the world around her than he, a human, has ever had.

"Look at dem bitches go, amirite?"

Startled, Ned turns his whole body to face the man towering over him, gleaming white teeth shining through a wide smile.

"I know ma girl Daisy sure loves dem odda bitches. Look a' dem, sniffing asses like it was a meet n' greet."

Ned says, "Or at a Yankee Candle Shoppe."

The big man roars out his amusement. He offers his hand out to Ned.

"Jeffery."

"Ned," and they both shake hands, Jeffery's cool against Ned's. Ned looks the man full in the face, and sees a jovial sparkle in his eyes, and a friendliness that inspires him to talk.

"My Nadia is that beagle over there, rolling in the grass. Who's your Daisy?"

"Ma girl is dat Rottie over there, shittin' on de Pug."

Ned looks over, aghast, but sees that Daisy, who is clearly not a puppy, sitting on top of another dog. Ned looks back at Jeffery, who is laughing even harder.

"Made ya look, didn I?"

"Yeah, you did, Jeffery."

Later, after handing Ned a copy of his business card, Jeffery whistles for his dog, releashes her, and walks away, waving goodbye to his new friend.

Ned looks down at the business card. Jeffery invited him over to a party at his house over the weekend. And, Ned thinks, what the hell just happened?

Time in the Well

by Darryl Price

Well it's no use. I belong behind bars. Not real bars, but bars that are walls, walls that are made out of row after row of huge, hulking trees. I want to come home to you, Doc. This real world stuff is not for me. I know you thought I could do it, but I'm just not made for the everyday living stuff. It scares me.

Put me in a circle any time.

All this jagged running around tires me out. I feel like a bumper car.

And I still miss someone.

That's never going away, is it? I'm just going to roll through life like a shell on a beach, subject to the whims of weather and not much else. Why? What did I do but love someone? Is love its own crazy punishment? I just want to be left alone – by love and everyone else.

Look, Doc, I admit I'm a long, strange case. I didn't ask for it. Well. I guess you didn't ask for it, for me, either, so maybe life's got it in for you, too.

At any rate, I know what you are going to say: you've got to get on with your life. Am I right? Okay, let's try it your way. But if I end up in a ditch somewhere, it's going to be your fault. No, I'm sorry, Doc, I don't mean to blame you. It's just that I don't feel a part of things any more.

At the grocery store I might as well be a vegetable or fruit.

At the movies I watch the chairs.

Outside I'm looking for the exit signs between trees to some other world than mine. The sun, the wind, these mean nothing to me, except to let me know they can slap me around.

Okay, things are spiraling as you put it so often and I've got to stop that kind of thinking in its tracks, so how about a story?

Once there was a little boy who could walk through walls. No one knew how he did it, not even the little boy. It just happened one day and then it always happened. At first all his friends took real delight in this fact. They made him do it over and over, but eventually they began to not ask to see this amazing trick of his. In fact they began to shun him for it. Soon he had no one to talk with or play with and this made the boy lonely. He would crawl into a wall and stay there for hours at a time. One day the little boy heard someone yelling for help, like this, "Help me, oh anyone, everyone, my girl has fallen down a well and can't climb back up!" Well, the boy sprang into action and walked right down through the walls of the old well and with only his arms and hands visible gently lifted the scared little girl to the top inch by inch until she was safe in her mother's arms once again. No one thanked the boy. They all left in a big rush, squeezing and kissing the missing child over and over again until the boy who could walk through walls was once again left completely alone. The stars came out before all his tears had dried. Suddenly there was a warm feeling in his left hand and he looked down to see the girl holding his hand. "Come on, Silly," she said, "everyone's waiting for you." After that, with the girl always nearby, the boy began to do all the normal things that boys his age do, and soon he forgot all about walking through walls. As a matter of fact he never brought it up again.

See there, Doc, a happy ending for all. Even if I can't have my own happy ending I'll give it to someone else.

Surely that's worth a readmission to the greatest show on earth. Let me know.

I'm spending way too much time in the well as it is.

Working on
My Jokes

by Teresa Burns Gunther

The orange sun lingers on Malibu's horizon. Susie's skin is tight from sun and sand; her eyes burn with saltwater tears. She hugs her knees, knocks her forehead against them, *fool, fool*. She sits up, dries her eyes and reminds herself that heartbreak is good for artistic development.

When she gave Steve a ride to LA to pursue his dream of acting she had no idea she'd end up in television. It was an old friend of Steve's who helped Susie landed a role in a soap: *nasty nurse*. She owes everything to Steve. The thought washes loneliness over her like the wave foaming up the shore. She wants to call Rachel, her go-to person in a crisis, though there's a good chance her cousin will say something to make her feel worse. Rachel's *on the spectrum*: odd to rude. Susie knows she doesn't mean it, that deep down she has a gentle heart; but her words can bite.

In July, while visiting Rachel in San Francisco, Susie met Steve and his tall cousin Kevin. A double cousin double date! Steve hugged Susie, called her adorable, and Susie recognized instant love on Fisherman's Wharf. They are so well matched: both from Indiana, blond, short, a little lost, and oh how they love to laugh. And Kevin was perfect for Rachel, who's 5'9" and says *tall men are in too short* supply *ha ha*. 6'3" and he even found Rachel's unfiltered comments amusing! That night, seeing the sights,

Susie was proud, for once she was the successful cousin bestowing favors.

Rachel told her she was crazy when she'd offered to drive Steve to LA, but Susie figured she had nothing to lose and Steve to gain. They'd had great fun cruising the California coast, surrounded in beauty, laughing, *happy, happy*. But when she'd crawled into his motel bed that first night in LA, telling him how she loved him – she cringes remembering – he'd jumped away, pulled a pillow between them, his long-lashed eyes wide with alarm, then pity. Oh they'd talked it all out. She understands now, though at first she tried to believe he was just confused and might change his mind. But today, Steve introduced her to his new boyfriend. Susie made happy noises, forcing her face to smile as she took pictures of them, grinning and holding each other's hands.

Susie watches the sun disappear and when the *scary scary* in her center starts squirming up she throws caution to the red horizon and calls Rachel. Comforted by her cousin's crisp voice she blurts out her news about Steve.

"When did you figure it out?" Rachel asks.

"You knew?" Susie asks. "Why didn't you tell me?"

"I thought it was obvious. But you always tell me not to rain on parades."

Susie considers this. As usual Rachel's right. She compliments her on her restraint and tells her about the sunset. Rachel steps outside and describes her own sky then asks about Susie's show: *As The Sperm Turns, ha ha*. Susie begins to regret calling but asks how it's going with Kevin. Rachel tells her they went out but he never called.

"Oh, no. What did you say?" Susie asks. Rachel's smart and beautiful, until she opens her mouth. It's not that her observations are wrong; they're just not always … necessary.

"Nothing. We had fun. I'm working on my jokes. That's my August resolution."

Susie groans.

"I can be funny. He laughed. Well," Rachel sniffs. "He *said* I was funny."

"Funny, good or funny … strange?"

Susie hurries home, shivering through the incoming fog, her worries shifted now to her awkward cousin.

After dinner, a shower, and a big glass of wine, Susie calls Steve.

"Hi Sugar," Steve says and Susie wishes, just this once, that he could sound the tiniest bit blue. She misses being the perky one. As they chitchat she looks around her small apartment noting the mess, as if Rachel and her disapproval are surveying it too. Steve teases her to reveal the next twist on her soap. He only watches it for her, which makes her love him even more. She laughs and scolds him and reminds herself they're *friends, friends.* Then she tells him about Rachel and Kevin.

"You shouldn't phone after 9:00 p.m."

"God, Rachel. Don't answer if you don't want to talk!" Susie snaps, then softens her tone and tells Rachel what she learned. "Kevin called but you never answered. He told Steve he even left a note on your porch."

"He's lying," Rachel says. "I have voice mail."

"Think about it. Why would he lie to Steve?"

"Good point," Rachel concedes, then she's quiet, Susie hears footsteps, a door opening, the dog barking, Rachel murmuring *Stella, Stella,* now scraping noises. "Okay," Rachel finally says. "His note's under my doormat, but I didn't get any phone messages."

"Well, maybe he got the number wrong," Susie says. "Stop being so logical, Dr. Spock." Rachel doesn't answer. Susie pictures her, head tilted, eyes moving, *thinking, thinking.* "Are you still there?"

"What should I do?" Rachel asks.

"You're asking me for advice?"

"Do you have any?"

"First tell me I did good."

"Why?" Rachel asks. "Nothing good has happened yet."

Susie laughs. "Just say it." They go back and forth, the tug of war lifts Susie's spirits.

"Ok. You did good," Rachel finally admits. "Now what should I do? Though why I'm asking you –"

"Stop," Susie says before Rachel's words destroy her little satisfaction. It's silly but she's savoring it all the same. "*Be smart. Figure it out,*" she says, mimicking Rachel's rational advice. Susie says she has to go practice her lines, realizing it's the first time with Rachel that she ever got to hang up first.

Morgana Malone and the Mystery of the Family Trust

by Matt Potter

"Don't look at them!" Jane says, tucking them under her chair.

I lean sideways in my seat and peer at her feet.

"Don't look at them, I said! I don't even know if I can stock them." Jane opens her folder on the table – "papyrus," she notes, "imported from the Maldives," – and taking out a business card, hands it to me.

NOT made in China, I read.

décor • clothing • collectibles, I read underneath.

… for the incredibly discerning, I read under that.

Then, *127a King William Road*.

"It's a nightmare getting stock not made in China," Jane says, picking up her chai latte. "A nightmare!"

She puts her cup down on the table again with a clink, rattling the plates left over from lunch – black quinoa and juju bean salad for her (the Monday lunch special) and haloumi, lettuce and drizzled macadamia oil focaccia for me – then slides a foot across the tiles and into the open.

"They're made in Tibet," she says, "of bamboo and yak leather. But which Tibet? *Chinese* Tibet or *Tibet* Tibet?"

The brown strips across her feet are crinkly, but so too is her skin – nothing covering them but the yak strips and blue with winter cold.

"And isn't the Dalai Lama from *Indian* Tibet?!" she continues. "These are the decisions I'm faced with. You are lucky you don't have a career or a husband or children or a new business to set up."

I gaze around the café, and sip my double strawberry milkshake through a straw as sugary strawberry syrup wafts up from the glass. Pale sun streams through the window, a reminder that spring – has it really been that long? – is not far away. Almond trees have already blossomed and the apricot tree in the back garden of the house I rent is smothered with white flowers. (Ludmilla, my former housemate, visited only yesterday and eyed the blossom, dollar signs spinning in her head as she calculated how many buckets she would need to strip the free fruit from the lower branches in a few months.)

I pull my cardigan closer across my breasts.

"But we need to talk about Mum and the cake shop," Jane adds. "When was the last time you saw her?"

I shake my head. "I've sort of been keeping to myself lately."

Jane runs her fingers through her hair. Which is naturally auburn, not unlike the colour I thought my hair might turn out when I had it dyed orange.

"Mum can't keep the cake shop up much longer," she says. "She's seventy-two and on her own and she needs help."

(When we were growing up I always wanted hair like Jane's. Everyone loved it. *Jane has such gorgeous hair, so thick and auburn and shiny*, was a comment her hair always earned. I wanted hair like hers, so everyone would envy me.

Now of course, with my dye growing out and the grey-brown roots expanding across my head, I have hair people feel sorry for.)

Jane clears her throat then looks straight at me.

"And you don't have a career or a husband or children or a new business to set up or even a job so you'll have to be the one to take over the cake shop because I *do* have a career and a husband and children and a new business to set up." Jane's breathes out. "*NOT made in China* won't set itself up, you know, and it's a business that I can well see will change the face of modern retailing."

I suck more double strawberry milkshake through the straw, my slurping noisy on the bottom of the glass. And then mention the unmentionable. "Why doesn't Mum sell the cake shop?"

Jane's mouth is a big 'O'. And then she gulps and collects her breath. "We'd never get what the cake shop is worth if we sold it in the current economic climate. And the cake shop is a family business. It'd be dreadful if it went out of the family. And let's face it Morgana, you stopped temping in January to work in your ex-husband's practice, and you left that *months* ago and *you're* not doing anything else so *you're* the obvious one to step in and help Mum." She purses her lips, and raises an eyebrow. "It's no different from when we were kids and we worked there on Saturday morning. She's seventy-two and on her own, and she needs help and it's time you stopped being so selfish and started thinking of others."

"But I'm seeing someone. We're talking about moving in together."

"And you know I've always had a head for business," Jane says, snapping the stud on her papyrus folder from the Maldives shut. "You know I know a lot about these things."

"So why don't *you* step in and work at the cake shop?" I suggest, assuming she's completely ignoring my news. "If anyone can keep it afloat, you can."

Jane sits back in her chair. "So who is this person you're seeing? Even though you're *sort of* keeping to yourself and don't have time to see your own mother."

Hmm, now I have to tell her.

"Well, you know," I say, "he has a bright future as a doctor and he's very good-looking and comes from a wealthy family and he's twenty-three."

"Twenty-three!" Jane says. "That's disgusting. You're old enough to be his mother." And a moment later, her eyes widen and raising an eyebrow again she looks directly at me and asks, "Is he good?"

A tall man with wavy brown hair and wearing a dark blue suit stands in the middle of the café and is looking at us.

"Is he good?" Jane asks again.

The tall man with wavy brown hair and wearing a dark blue suit is now two tables away.

"Are you just going to ignore me, Morgana?"

I snap my head to look at her because she never calls me Morgana and today she's called me that twice. I changed my name to Morgana a decade and a half ago and she's never –

"Susan?"

"Yes," we both say.

I look across the table at Jane. Who is now touching the ends of her naturally auburn hair.

The tall man with wavy brown hair and wearing a dark blue suit says, "You're both Susan?"

"No," we both say.

"Susan is my former name," I say, sounding very formal.

"And Susan is my new name," Jane tells him, and then looking at me across the table, she points at the business card she gave me and says, "for business purposes. It's on my card." And she flips over the card and there it is plain as day, *Susan Green-Baye*, her new name, which is actually my old name, with her husband's surname hyphened on the end.

"But *Susan Green* is my name."

118

"It *was* your name but it's not now, it's mine." And she smiles up at the tall man.

No one says anything. Perhaps the tall man's name is Susan Green too.

The tall man looks at me and then at Jane. "So which Susan used to be married to Grigor Smiroveich?" he asks.

"*She* did," the new Susan Green hyphen Baye says. "That was a looong time before I was ever Susan."

The tall man smiles. "Then this is for you," he says, and places a white envelope in front of me. "Have a nice day."

He hasn't cornered the next table over and I know what it is.

"What is it?" my sister (it's easier to call her that now) asks.

I pick the envelope up and without opening it, start ripping it into pieces. "Just Grigor still trying to get more money out of me for his cancelled wedding," I say.

"Don't look to me if you need money because I haven't got any," she says. "I have a husband and children and a business to support." She waves her hand in the air to signal a waitress.

I stare at the envelope and its contents, now a messy white paper pile on the table.

"It's all part of my business strategy," the new Susan continues. "Which I would not expect you to understand because you don't have a head for business like I do."

My eyes blur. She's expecting me to say something but I'm not going to say anything. What I want to do is shove the messy pile of paper down her throat and make her eat it.

"I went to a business specialist – she's very New-Agey – and she said *Jane* was not a good name for a businesswoman but *Susan* is."

The words are stuck in my throat. I breathe out and the paper flutters on the table. I can't look at my sister. So I look past her and out the window and I see Seth standing on the footpath: he with the bright future as a doctor who's very good-looking with high cheekbones on a thin face and short dark hair atop deep brown eyes and comes from a wealthy family and is twenty-three. I'd asked him to meet me after lunch. And my heart lurches inside my ribcage because, if ever I need rescuing, it's now.

"I had to take a bottle of sand from a place that's special to me but I didn't have any time to go to the beach so I just took a bucket and spade to the local kindergarten and got it from their sand pit. She's a sand reader."

I pick up my handbag from the spare chair beside me.

"And you weren't using your old name any more and it's a free country," she adds.

I stand up and look down at her. "I was hoping to start a new life again and I thought it might be nice to start by getting my old name back."

A waitress watches me as, high heels clacking on the floor, I head towards the door and a grinning Seth standing outside. I smile as I stop at the counter.

"Please send the lunch bill to this address," I say, handing the waitress the *NOT made in China* business card my sister gave me. "And mark it, *Attention: Susan*."

Tuesday

26

August
2014

Q

by Gary Percesepe

How did I meet her?

We were both members of an online community, where writers from around the world would post their stories, poems, and essays, and comment on the writing of others. I cannot remember if she commented on my work first, or if I commented on hers. But I do remember reading one of her stories, which was an alphabet of desire. She wrote as someone who knew about the messiness of human relationships, and sex – connected and disconnected from love – but more, she seemed to understand the smallest calibrations of the human heart, how restless we are until we find – what? What is it that we are looking for? I didn't know either. But reading her stories, I began to name what it is that I wanted in this life by her name, Q. I wanted her. I didn't know her. But her writing knew me, had interrogated me, flushed me out, and called to me.

Having someone take the time to read your work, and make a telling comment, one that strikes at the core of what you intended to say, what you meant, someone who gets every feint, every gesture, every subtle characterization, every plot point, every word choice – is so rare. Everyone reads and writes from somewhere – all writing is contextual. Every writer wants to believe that he or she writes for some*body*.

John Updike once famously described his imagined or ideal reader as a teenage boy who happens upon one of his books on the dusty shelves of some library one afternoon looking for literary adventure. Updike found me in this way. But nothing could prepare me for Q, who somehow came to me through my work. She read me all the way through; she read me in every way that a reader can read you, and get you.

Being read by someone you do not know is strange. She sits somewhere with your work in her hands (on her screen?) in a place, in a time, in a setting that is unknown to you. Then one day, magically, she posts a comment on your work. You see her picture (as on Facebook), a picture of the person who has commented on a piece of writing so deep in your heart, so interior, that it is embarrassing to you even that you have posted it, but now here is this woman, a stranger, really, an amazing beautiful stranger (from her picture) who is telling you that she loves your work which, let us imagine, took you two decades to write, it was so painful, and let's say it was a portion of a memoir, or later a poem that you tossed off, let's say she read your poem of New York longing.

And off to the side of my poem Q wrote:

> an anthem shaped to fit into the city's skyline: love it. The juxtapositions of images uniquely yours and full of yearning. Horn & Hardart may never return, but won't you come home to us, Gary?

Right there, with one comment on a poem, she took an axe to the frozen sea inside and she had me then, though I didn't know it at the time. It would be a month before I met her, for drinks in Manhattan when I was in town. We met at an Italian restaurant I had liked once upon a time, but on this night there was construction outside and the restaurant was empty and there was only the two of us and we twittered away, two writers chirping, and I had been interested in another woman, also in New York, and still had a wife at home, and wanted to be (and was) on my best behavior, but we went on talking, and I thought, she is easy to talk to, she is full of heart, she is small, petite, I could fit my arms around her waist and carry her off, and the waiter kept asking and I kept declining to eat until exasperated they wanted to close the restaurant at 8 pm – this was Midtown Manhattan! – and Q exploded at the manager (I watched, amused – 90% heart, I calculated, the rest, fire), who responded by flicking the lights on and off, and just like that she had done it, what hadn't happened in so long, she ignited another fire in me (I had been in love three times in my life), one that smoldered for a month, until we met again on the roof of her building and she walked me through the edits she had made to my novel and I tried to listen while I studied the shape of her face, strands of her dark hair blowing in the breeze on a cool day in May. Then, in June, I waited for her outside a trendy restaurant in Greenwich Village. A pretty girl sat next to me on a bench outside the restaurant. She was vaguely European and smoked furiously on a small cigarette while we watched the weather. A storm was approaching. The wind was picking up, and the sky darkening. The Euro girl asked if I was waiting for someone and I said yes. Then I saw Q, walking toward me. I got up and went to her.

I keep trying to go to her. But there doesn't seem to be a way to be together, or at least no way that I know. The time is out of joint. No way is open.

Samford, a Motel 6 Couch, and the Blonde Woman

by Nathaniel Tower

Samford is feeling rather horny, which is a good thing because he has found himself on top of a blonde-haired woman on a couch in the lobby of a Motel 6. There is no one behind the desk, and the blonde has her hands down his pants. It's the first time he's been with a blonde woman. At least he thinks it is.

The blonde is quick and efficient. She lifts her skirt and has his real human penis inside what he thinks must be her real human vagina within seconds. It all happens so quick that he's not even sure how he ended up with his boner inside the hottest woman he's ever seen in a Motel 6.

She doesn't scream or moan or grunt or anything. It's the most silent act of fornication ever. They might as well be in a library or a church. The springs in the worn-out couch don't squeak or creak. Samford constantly looks over at the desk to see if the concierge – if they even call them that at a Motel 6 – is back there watching him. He doesn't think the concierge will break them up or call the cops. Hell, the scumbag would probably video tape it and have the whole event up on YouTube before Samford even blows his load.

At the precise moment Samford thinks about blowing his load, his load blows inside the blonde. The blonde smiles and nods and pushes him gently to indicate that he may get off her. There is no indication whatsoever that she has enjoyed herself even in the slightest, but Samford has to ask. "Was that good for you?" To his knowledge, this is the first thing he has ever said to her.

She keeps the smile on her face. "It wasn't bad for me." Then she pulls his pants back on for him and drops her skirt. They both sit up on the couch just as the concierge walks in.

"Do you need a room?" the concierge asks.

Samford looks at the woman in a panic. Will she want to share a room with him after that?

"Nope," she says before he can say anything. "He already fucked me, right here on this couch. In fact, his sperm has already swum up and fertilized one of my eggs. I can feel the baby growing in my belly."

Samford half-swallows a laugh, but he really does find it funny. He could see himself with this woman.

The concierge doesn't laugh. "Don't fuck with me," he says. "I'll have you two thrown in jail. Now, do you want a room, or not?"

"I'm not fucking with you." The blonde smiles. "I was fucking with him." She slaps Samford right on the thigh and squeezes, his erection returning even though the touch isn't affectionate.

The concierge picks up the phone. "That's it. I'm calling the cops."

The blonde stands up. "I wouldn't do that if I were you." Samford expects her to pull out a weapon, but there's no way she could have one on her.

The concierge begins dialing. Samford looks back and forth between the woman and the hotel worker. The blonde's stomach gurgles and begins to expand, within moments the size of a watermelon. "What the fuck?" the concierge says and the phone slips out of his hands.

The blonde's stomach continues to expand. She props one leg up on the couch. "Get ready, Sam," she says. Samford glances up her skirt and sees an arm emerging from her unpantied crotch.

"What the hell?"

"Just get ready!" she shouts. It isn't angry or even really a panic.

Samford holds his arms out, ready to catch whatever is coming out.

"No, just get out of the way."

Samford dives on the floor and watches a full-grown human emerge from her vagina. The thing slides out but isn't goopy at all like he would expect. Then again, it hasn't had much time to ferment in there.

The full-grown man hits the couch first and then bounces on the floor. The blonde lets out a relieved sigh. The concierge sprints out of the Motel 6. Samford stares at the man who possesses every single one of Samford's features down to the tiniest imperfections.

The man stands. "What the fuck are you looking at?" he says to Samford. The voice is familiar, but Samford doesn't think he sounds quite like that.

The blonde looks at Samford and smiles. "Your work here is done. You can go now."

Samford stands and stares at her. He wants to say something, to ask if it hurt, to ask why him, to ask if he needs to stay and raise it with her. Then he hears sirens approaching. Questions will only lead to answers he doesn't want. He bursts through the Motel 6 doors and sprints off into the night.

Kununurra

by Kimberlee Smith

She's been on the road for a month, my mum Maybell, on a trip that wouldn't take anyone else in the world more than a fortnight, and that'd be with plenty of stops along the way. She's traveling from our home in Sydney to the outskirts of Kununurra in the Kimberley region, where, she's been told by members of her old congregation after belabored inquiries, that Brother Tom Bend set his sights on finding a particularly sinful and barbaric aboriginal tribe he believes he can save through prayer and deliverance. Brother Tom is her ex-husband and my daddy. We hadn't seen him in a handful-plus of years.

Mum never did explain why. Maybe by the grace of God she'll find him, and I cannot wait to find out what stirred her up to do such a thing. For whatever reason she's searching him down, her curiosity bled over to me and I'm getting impatient following her as she travels with my bub, Etheline, who's exactly seven and one-half months old today. I'm not understanding Mum's tactics of stalling a trip that she started out hell-bent on finishing in record time. If she hadn't a burning need to get to him as fast as possible she never would have traveled eight hours her first day on the road wearing an adult diaper so she didn't have to stop at a dunny.

The closer she gets to him, the more side trips she takes, meandering across the country to see everything there is to see and even what I would consider a colossal waste of time.

She's driving my old Jackaroo that has over 392,000 kilometers on it. The petrol gauge is stuck on one-third full no matter how full the tank is. And no one either bothered to or, I hope, wanted to pop out the Tom Waits tape I was listening to the day before I died. Since Mum turned on the music to drown out the silence of the drive, she's been signing along with every song, knows all the words. But she most loves his version of *Waltzing Matilda*. It was her favorite song before hearing Tom Waits sing it, and I don't think she knew he was my favorite singer. I wish so bad that right now I could be there riding shotgun along with her. The longer I've been gone, the closer to her and the bub I feel.

and the ghosts that sell memories
want a piece of the action anyhow
go waltzing matilda, waltzing matilda
you'll go a-waltzing matilda with me …
… and his ghost may be heard
as you pass by that billabong
who'll come a-waltzing matilda with me

The lyrics go more or less like that. Not the way they were originally written, and I don't believe she's even hearing the words she's singing, but she knows them perfectly, each and every one.

After driving for eight hours, Mum stopped at Trilby station in Louth where she fished along the banks until the sun went down, unaware that a toxic phosphorescent bloom had killed off most of the fish this past summer and the ones that remained were horribly poisonous (she thankfully didn't hook one fish but had an extra gin and lime cordial that night, "Bob's your uncle!" she exclaimed to herself with too much hilarity as she poured herself another, while the bub slept straight through it, thankfully), then slowed her pace on day two, driving half the distance where she explored a used-books store and spent a dollar on a copy of *The Thorn Birds*.

She stopped at the Bandicoot Bar Hotel for the night and ended up staying for two, getting to know the locals, of which there weren't many. Most folks were like Mum, passers-through on their way somewhere else. The first night, Mum brought Etheline in her pram into the pub, and fed her mushy peas and fish she pulverized with the tines of her fork, taking extra care to pluck out a few bones that were as thin as a strand of hair. The bub absolutely loved it, bobbing her head like a cockatoo and clapping. Mum read her new book while she ate a cheeseburger with fried egg to soak up the gin and lime cordials she drank as daintily as she could, for appearances' sake. They had such a fine time and slept so well, snuggled up on a mattress as small as a camp bed, Mum decided to do it again the following night.

It took her over a week to reach Uluru, and she stayed there for *three* nights. She bought mozzie nets to cover her and the bub's faces, and the bub kept fussing to pull hers off. She was trying to eat the mozzies. This is not a good sign. But Mum knew that the venom that killed me had surged through Etheline's bloodstream and gave her a taste for insects and animals in general. She gave in and took the net off the bub and let her have her way with the mozzies. Etheline became so adept at catching them and popping them in her mouth and grinding them down with her slippery pink gums that Mum wasn't bothered by the pests anymore and she took off her net as well.

§

By the time they made it to Broome, they'd been three weeks on the road. I'm getting a feeling that Mum is procrastinating because she's apprehensive about seeing Brother Tom after all these years, how he's going to react, but more so how *she'll* feel. She loved him as much as the sun, the moon, the stars, and everything in between. That's what she used to tell him and me. I kept my mouth shut and never corrected her that the fact is the sun is a star, because that's not important. What is important is that I believe she *never* stopped loving him that much. She's afraid and I don't blame her one bit.

Today is the last of five days they've spent on Cable Beach. The bub is transfixed, watching the camels lope along the shoreline. Mum brought the baby backpack along for hiking and whatnot. *Whatnot* at Cable Beach means strapping Etheline into the backpack and taking a camel ride at sunset along the beach for an hour. The bub lays her head on Mum's shoulder and smiles and coos for the whole bumpy hour they ride along. It's one of the most beautiful things I've ever seen. All the tourists are taking pictures of the unlikely pair of travelers, promising to send copies back to Mum when their travels end. The bloke who runs the operation there asks Mum if he could use their picture in a poster for advertising purposes and Mum blushes like a schoolgirl.

"You hear that, you cheeky little monkey? We're going to be famous!" she says to Etheline, who pats Mum on both cheeks and puckers her lips to kiss Mum all over her face.

"Da, da, da*mum,*" the bub says, sounding as if she's imitating the drumbeat in a parade.

Mum's face lights up as bright as the fireworks over Sydney Harbour on New Year's Eve and she turns to Hugo, which is the name of the bloke in charge.

"You hear that? Her voice cracks on the last word and she's got a smile as wide as the sea. "She said my name. First time. She called me grandmum."

"So how you going now?" Hugo says, then laughs and shakes his head.

"Better than I been in a long while. Tell you that much. I live for this little one, I do," Mum says.

"She's a doll, no doubt you do. You two traveling alone, hey? Giving her mum and dad a break?" he asks.

"Naw. I wish. Her mum and dad, well, they passed right when she was born. It's the two of us, just us two," Mum says. She looks over at the bub, who is reaching out to pet the camel they rode. He dips his head toward her and makes a motorboat noise as his floppy lips rumble.

"His name is Ghan. I can tell he really likes you, darlin'," says Hugo to the bub. "Not true with all folks. He's a discriminating camel."

Hugo looks at Mum, who is squinting her eyes and has a hangdog face as she looks right to the sinking sun. The sky is the color of fire and amethysts.

"Sorry to hear that, ma'am. Sorry about your loss," says Hugo as he moves closer to Ghan and rubs his neck, but Ghan is leaning down to Etheline.

Mum doesn't acknowledge this. It's understandable. I'm surprised she said anything about the accidents, she hasn't told a soul about it. The thought of it must be painful enough for her; I cannot imagine her mustering the strength to say it out loud, *My daughter died from a lethal snakebite right before the bub was taken from her womb. Emergency Caesarean. It was just me and her widower, Dean, and the bub. A few months after, Dean was killed in a plane crash. Transporting those snakes that he bought and sold for business. That trip was the one he finally was able to get rid of the coral snake that killed my daughter. He died on the way home to us.*

That's just not a conversation you can have with anyone. I bet it'd be easier to talk about it with a stranger than someone who knew us, but that's relative. I can't imagine a person even revisiting that story in their own head, never mind enunciating it out loud.

"How 'bout that, ma'am. Ghan likes the bub more than he likes me, and I live with him!" says Hugo.

"She has a way with animals taking kindly to her," says Mum.

Hugo pulls on Ghan's reins and Ghan makes a squeal in protest then gives in. Hugo makes a comment about feeding time and says "Git" to the camel, who looks up at him and follows him back to the stable.

Mum carries the bub in her arms to the car and straps her into her safety seat, then wipes the sand off the bottom of her own shoes. She leans into the back of the car and whispers, "I love you, Etheline. As much as the sun, the moon, the stars, and everything in between." Her eyes get all misty and she is as happy as I've seen her since I left.

This evening, after one more hour on the road, they hit the mark of traveling for an entire month and finally enter Kununurra. Mum drives along the Ord River and then through about forty kilometers of farmland. The air dark as wet ink is dry and warm and smells like mango and sandalwood. Stars pepper the sky. Etheline sleeps with a smile spread across her face. Her pale blonde eyelashes flutter from colorful dreams.

Mum talks to herself out loud.

"After brekkie, I'ma put Etheline in her finest dress ... the one the color of the inside of a shell. All that pretty cotton lace around the hem. And white socks with lace to match. And shiny little white booties with the ribbon ties." She laughs, not heartily but wistfully.

"Soles of those shoes never gonna wear out. By the time she's walkin,' she won't fit in them anymore. Maybe I'ma get them bronzed. Put them up on the mantle. I'ma put on my best dress, too, now that I'm thinking of it."

I think it's time. I think she's ready.

Trypophobia

by Vanessa Weibler Paris

Every day I go to work and leave Iris behind. Home, alone.

What I know about Iris: She's fascinated by bones. Broken bones. My bones.

What I know about Iris: Like her floral namesake, she is beautiful and bewitching.

What I know about Iris: She is the first woman who has kissed me. Who has said she loves me.

What I know: She loves her art more than she'll ever love me. Or herself.

What I don't know about Iris: Is what I don't know about Iris. Yet. Or ever.

"What will you do today?" I ask this morning, as I'm drinking my coffee – lightened with skim milk, per Iris, instead of my former heavy cream. I've spent my life trying to gain, to stop being Slim Jim and finally become Jamie, but Iris likes me this way.

"I'm working on a new series," she says.

"More bones?" I ask.

"In a sense," she tells me.

"Broken?"

"In a way."

"What's it called?"

"Trypophobia," she says, licking blackstrap molasses from the blade of a serrated kitchen knife as she does every morning. "But that's all I will say. I can't talk about it until it's finished."

I go to work and spend my breaks online, learning the word and finding the pictures of the holes. Lotus pods and honeycombs and hair plugs. I take my phone into the bathroom and crouch in the stall, searching more. Crumpets and lava rocks and Surinam toads. Bone marrow.

Bone marrow.

I click through page after page after page, enlarging them. Zooming. Sweating. Goosebumping. Someone flushes and I grab the toilet paper roll, leaving a damp spindly handprint behind.

All day long, I can only think of the holes.

I sit in meetings and talk on the phone, and shiver: envisioning the holes. I drive home and kiss Iris hello and sit down to something low-fat and low-calorie for dinner, and shudder: imagining the holes.

"Drink your water," Iris says over grilled salmon and steamed asparagus, pushing my glass closer as though it's out of reach. "You don't drink enough water."

"I'll drink it," I say, and I do. And then I drink another. And I wonder how it stays in. I am full of holes, my ears and my nose and my penis and my pores. There's water everywhere, I think, pouring a third glass. And it keeps seeping in and leaking out of everything.

I drink my water, imagining Iris filling a dropper with bleach and squeezing it drop by drop by drop onto my bare skin. The flesh would sizzle as each hole formed, and she'd do it carefully, systematically, starting at the center and working her way out outward like a flower blooming. It would burn down to the bone, making marrow external.

Would it hurt, or feel like relief?

Eventually I'd be covered with them, round and neat like office hole-punches, and liquid would start to ooze out. It might be red or it might be yellow or it might be the clear water I'd drunk. It might be fears or it might be feelings or it might be words I can never say.

I chew my fish and sip my drink and listen to Iris hum. It takes me a few seconds to recognize 'Coin-Operated Boy' by the Dresden Dolls.

I picture a lotus pod, riddled with holes like a showerhead. The cluster of seeds, loose but secure. Bulging, sharp-tipped, staring like eyes and poking like breasts.

"Are you okay?" Iris asks. She reaches out, touches my arm and I shriek.

Eli Dangott

by Joanne Jagoda

"Liat, are you there? *Ma nishma?*"

"I'm good. We are about ten minutes from you sitting in a Starbucks on Judah St. How's it going Eli? Still up on the pole?"

"Liat, you sound just like an American teenager."

"I've been studying Cassie's voice, and you know I'm good with accents."

"It's blazing hot up here and I'm sweating like a pig in this utility man get-up. This must be one of the five hot days of the year in this city. I wish I was at the Beach in Tel Aviv with Dafne. I'm sick of listening to Cassie and Robin bicker, but I guess that's what teens do. The shopping trip to Stanford is a 'go'. Damon has his team in place. We've been monitoring him closely. Everybody ready?"

"Yes, I've got my transmitters set in place. Travis and the boys are waiting for your signal to take Cassie to the safe house. And don't forget your credentials. Anne will want to see them."

"May I help you? Do we have a gas leak?"

"Anne Donaldson?"

"Yes, that's me. What do you want?" Her voice is sharp and suspicious.

"Anne, please call Cassie and Robin." She opens the door but not all the way. She is looking at me as though she recognizes me but can't place where she has seen me.

"Girls, come to the door, NOW."

When they hear their mother's no-nonsense tone, they join her silently by her side. They are puzzled why a tall, olive-skinned, sweaty utility worker is standing at their door.

"My name is Eli Dangott. I'm not a utility worker. I'm the grandson of Holocaust survivors and a member of the Mossad, the Israeli equivalent of the Secret Service. Here, you can verify who I am."

Anne scrutinizes my identification in its leather holder and quickly reads the letter from Homeland Security which vouches for me. She shakes her head and hands the credentials back.

"I don't understand. What do you want with us?"

"Let's sit, and if you don't mind a glass of water would be appreciated." I take off my hard hat and strip off the neon vest and gloves and wipe my sweaty face with a bandana.

"Thank goodness I can take this stuff off. It's hot out there today." I pull out my cell and send a quick text to my team: *We're on. Get moving!*

Cassie hands me a glass of water, and I take a long sip. "Let me start by telling you why I'm here. I work closely with your Homeland Security as a liaison from the state of Israel in matters of national security that affect both of our countries."

Robin interrupts, "Are you a spy? Like James Bond?"

She doesn't get the urgency of the situation. My team is coming to get Cassie in ten minutes, and I need to get everyone on board. My tone is harsh. "Let me go on. I've been closely tracking the movements of David Lewis, whose name is actually *Damon Southeby*, since Interpol flagged Homeland Security when he entered the country from Canada using a fake passport. The state of Israel was alerted when it became apparent from his emails and phone chatter he was going to obtain the plans for your grandfather's Project Octopus by kidnapping Cassie and holding her for ransom. Israel has to be sure that Project Octopus doesn't land in the hands of our enemies."

Anne is incredulous and her face is reddening. She stands up and points to the door. "I don't believe any of this. Maybe you should leave NOW."

The twins giggle out of nervousness. Robin tells her mother, "Mom let him go on."

Anne stares at me. "Wait. I do know you. You look really familiar. I remember now. You were in Calistoga. Next to me at the pool. I noticed you watching me."

"Yes, I was there tracking you and your uh … David. Other members of my team were keeping a close eye on your girls. We've been tempted several times to whisk you all away into a safe house, but we felt it best to let this all play out."

Anne grabs a heavy pottery vase from the coffee table and stands up ready to hurl it at me. Her instinct is to take the girls and run out of the house.

"Why have you been following us? Are we in danger?"

Robin pipes up. "What's this about anyway?"

"Anne, put the vase down and sit. You, Robin and Cassie are the targets of an elaborate plot but we are doing everything possible to keep you safe. You know that George Donaldson's company has developed Project Octopus. There are many foreign interests who would do anything to get those plans."

Robin interrupts again, "But Grandpa's work has nothing to do with us."

"I'm afraid it does. Let me be frank with you. Damon Southeby is a foreign agent working for a terrorist conglomerate who wants those plans at any cost. His idea all along was to get close to your family and kidnap one of you girls as ransom."

Robin points to herself and has a triumphant smirk on her face, "See … I knew it. I knew it. There was something off about *David* or whatever the hell his name is."

"Your instincts were right Robin." Anne lets out a pitiful sob, stands up and runs into the bathroom.

I hear her retching. I knew this would be a shock for her. Cassie follows her mother into the bathroom to check on her while Robin eyes me suspiciously. After ten minutes, she returns wan and spent with Cassie holding her hand tightly.

She sniffles, "How could I not know he was a phony. I thought I was in love with him."

"Anne, Damon is one of the slickest agents in the world. He cultivated you and studied your habits like a cunning hunter and preyed on your vulnerability. Your family was the perfect target. There are Homeland Security agents briefing George and Lillian now. Our engineers in Israel have developed fake blueprints which will be used for the ransom. We have an agent we have brought in from Israel to take your place, Cassie. You are the one who is going to be kidnapped."

Cassie gasps and Robin grabs her sister's hand and doesn't let go. "How did you and that horrible man know everything about what we were doing today? That's creepy."

"I don't have time to explain more right now Cassie."

Anne has little blotches of color on her cheeks. "That … lying, scheming asshole. I want him to be caught. What can we do?"

"We have to work quickly. The shopping trip to Stanford will take place as planned, but Cassie's double will stand in for her. She will go in the car with you, Anne, and Robin. She will enter the Apple store supposedly to select her new computer, but Anne and Robin you will leave her there and go to Macy's. We suspect the Apple store is where the snatch is going to take place. Robin, mention you need to get stuff at Macy's on the drive over, and you need your mom's help. Damon has your car bugged. Be aware of that. You and our agent should argue like you usually do with your sister."

Robin looks at her sister with tears in her eyes. Cassie is white and silent.

Anne, Cassie and Robin start when they hear knocking. Eli opens the door. A young woman walks in who is a dead ringer for Cassie at a quick glance: auburn curly hair, wearing denim shorts just like she has on, an identical San Francisco Giants tee shirt, and is her exact height and similar build.

"My name is Liat, and I will be taking your place, Cassie."

Cassie is sobbing, "I … I … don't want you to get hurt."

"Cassie, you don't have to be concerned about my safety. I'm well-trained, an expert in martial arts and have hidden transmitters in my shoe, my bra, my necklace and even the bracelet that David got your for graduation."

Robin pipes up, "You even sound like Cassie."

Eli interrupts, "Liat will brief you on the plans for today. Cassie, pack a few things. We are taking you to a safe house overnight."

"What?" Anne and Robin answer together.

"Cassie will be perfectly safe, enjoying a nice swimming pool, video games, movies and will be guarded 24/7."

Liat stands up like she is leading a class. "This is the plan …"

Gingerhead Man

by h. l. nelson

Dear Diary,

I may have really fucked up this time. I just got back from a night at the karaoke bar ... and somewhere else afterward. I'm in my art room, not wanting to get into bed. What the hell am I thinking? But I suppose it was so pathetic that Brandon would probably just laugh. He mentioned two nights ago that he hasn't felt the same way about me for a while, so I think I'm scared he's going to ask for a divorce. The conversation started when he saw some pictures I took of the girls and me at that StrollerFit class. Thank God he doesn't know about the Piss Perfume escapade. I don't know, he hasn't said anything, but he may be snooping around in my art room. Anyway, knowing that we're having issues ... why I did what I did, I have no idea.

The karaoke bar is in this Mexican restaurant. Being so far from Mexico, you can imagine how horrible the food is. All the cooks are Asian. I'm not sure why we go. We eat the chips and salsa, which isn't horrible, and drink the bottled domestics (no tap, of course) while lazily watching the untalented singers and their hideous renditions of 'Pour Some Sugar on Me' and 'Love Shack'.

So the girls and I were buzzing, eating chips, and chatting and a very red-headed, suited man I had never seen there before stepped up to the mic. He cleared his throat and the first strains of 'How Do I Live?' by Leann Rimes flitted through the restaurant. I elbowed Robin and pointed at the stage. She rolled her eyes and took a swig of her Shiner Bock. I smiled and turned back to the stage. I wasn't going to admit it, but I was intrigued by this ginger stranger and wanted to see what he could do.

The song began and he was surprisingly good. He had his eyes closed for most of the performance and really belted it out. And he got quite a bit of applause, whoops, and whistles. And not just from me. When he was finished, he turned red due to the applause, kept swiping his hand over his sweaty, receding hairline. As he exited the stage, I caught his eye and reflexively smiled at him before I could look away. He had a nice smile.

"You like that guy?" Robin smirked. Julie looked back and forth between us.

"Oh, I don't know. He's all right. Kinda sweaty." I turned back to the bar, trying to look nonchalant, and took a sip of my beer.

"Uh huh, I saw how you were looking at him and I –" she teased, but stopped because Julie had spilled her drink down her shirt.

"Dammit, Julie! Are you that drunk already? Ugh. Joan, I'm gonna go help her clean her drunk ass up. Hold our seats."

"Okay," I said, as they swayed to the bathroom. Obviously, they were both sauced and I would need to keep my wits about me so I could drive us. I also knew that Robin would try to pick a fight soon if we didn't get some liquor in her.

Two giggly teenage girls were giving 'Like a Virgin' a go onstage and I was checking my cell for messages from Brandon or the kids when I felt someone to my left. I looked over and Gingerhead was standing there, looking like a deer about to be creamed. I smiled quick at him, but he stood in the same position with the same facial expression for a good 15 seconds. I was starting to get creeped out and glanced about for an escape route in case he started stroking my hair and making goose calls.

"Sorry, hi. Do you mind if I grab this seat?" he said.

"Uh, hi there. Sure." I could grab my bottle and knock him over the head if he started dancing the Macarena on me. God help him if he did.

"I, uh, noticed you enjoyed my performance," he said, signaling the bartender. "Scotch and soda, please. No lime."

He seemed saner when he ordered his whiskey without lime, so I relaxed, leaning back in my chair.

"I did. You sang it well. I'm not a Rimes fan, but I liked your rendition." I noticed a lighter, circular area of skin on his ring finger. Pointing it out, I asked, "Are you married?"

"Oh, no. I'm a, uh, widower."

I got the impression he was lying, and I was a tad tipsy, so I said, "Haha, good one. The ol' 'I'm a widower'. How's that one working for you?" and I turned away from him. I mean, really, I was a total hypocrite. Here I was with no ring on my finger – I'd taken it off after the conversation with Brandon – and I was giving this red-haired stranger hell.

"Oh, wow. Uh, I'm sorry. I didn't mean to make it sound like a line. I don't really use lines. I hope you have a good night."

He turned to leave, but I grabbed his arm. "Look, I'm sorry. I'm bad at this. Please, stay."

"Okay. So yeah, I'm bad at this, too. I've never really dated much at all. My wife and I were high school sweethearts. Together for 31 years." He looked down at his beer and I could tell he was trying not to get emotional. But he looked up and smiled at me. I would be lying if I said it didn't make my heart beat quicker.

Before I could say "bad Mexican food," I had hiked it to the bathroom to check on the girls – Julie was sick and needed to get home. Robin was pissed but didn't want to leave Julie, so I grabbed a cab for them. Then, somehow I ended up following Gingerhead out of the bar. He never once asked if I was married. He probably assumed I wasn't, since I made such a big stink.

I felt guilty. I'd never cheated on Brandon before. But sadly, more overwhelming than the guilt was utter nervousness. Walking to my car, I tried to remember if I'd shaved everything, put on enough deodorant, worn sexy panties. I came to the conclusion that the panties I had on weren't my sexiest, but also weren't the granny panties I wear when I have my period. And the few-day-old stubble down south would just have to do. I could casually tell him I was growing it out for a waxing. Or like one of those long, thin beards that guys sometimes braid. Braided pubes … Okay, no, I wouldn't tell him that.

I sniffed my armpits while driving and wrinkled my nose. Ew. I had some perfume in my purse. Sitting at the traffic light, I sprayed it then so I wouldn't douse his bathroom in the stuff. Digging in your purse for something while driving and then putting it on while driving is a skill, let me tell you. My car smelled like it was looking for a good time.

We got to his place, a small apartment on the east side. Not a horrible neighborhood, but certainly not the best. He helped me out of my car, which was sweet. Then we hiked it up to his 3rd floor apartment. I was hoping the walk would dissipate some of the perfume, but the heat from my underarms only made it stronger.

His place was immaculately clean. Way cleaner than any bachelor's pad I'd ever seen. I figured his wife must have trained him pretty well. He offered me a drink and I went to the kitchen with him to help him make them. You know, just in case he was actually a weirdo. Though I was now in his apartment, alone with him. So, perhaps I wasn't the smartest person in the world. I glanced around for pillows and lampshades made of human skin.

He poured me a vodka on the rocks and made a scotch for himself. We took our drinks to his living room. I didn't want to set mine down anywhere, due to the cleanliness. I didn't see any coasters, so I just held it. It was warm in the apartment; the ice in my drink had started to melt. Condensation dripped on my blouse.

I could tell he wasn't used to bringing women to his place. His forehead was shining again, and he kept tripping over his words.

"So, Joan, what do you do for money – I mean, career-wise?"

"Well, I stay at home mostly. My kids are teenagers, so I look after the house."

"Oh, uh, are you independently wealthy? I mean, sorry, that's none of my business."

He looked uncomfortable and took a big drink from his glass. He fumbled it and most of it ended up on his shirt-front. His face burned bright red.

"Dammit! My wife bought me this shirt – I mean, it's a favorite. Let me go clean up."

After he loped to the bathroom, I contemplated leaping off of his balcony. Instead, I moved over to his record collection. He had quite a few. I saw many singers who I admire, including what looked like a Miles Davis that I had never seen before. I couldn't tell for sure because it was in a semi-opaque plastic cover, so I put my drink down on the shelf and took the record out to get a better look. I was admiring it when he returned and said, "Oh, no! That can't be out!"

Startled, I bumped the shelving unit, spilling the contents of my glass all over his albums.

"Oh, shit!" we both yelled in unison. It was the most in-sync thing we achieved the entire night. He ran to the kitchen and came back with a few dish towels, handed me one, then grabbed records off the shelf and wiped them. I helped. I would have laughed at the scene if I hadn't been appalled at spilling the drink.

"Oh my god, I'm so sorry," I said, as he surveyed the damage. A few sleeves were bubbling up in places.

"Hey, it was a mistake." He was surprisingly calm about the whole ordeal, which turned me on. Obviously, I was still tipsy.

"I know how I can make it up to you," I said, and sidled up to his side. His face blossomed red again.

Thirty minutes later, it was over and he was crying. Let me back up. I don't mean the sex was over. We didn't even get that far. We kissed a little – awkwardly, I might add. Then he put his hand on my right boob in the typical go-for-the-tits-way-too-early move that many guys are so fond of. And he just burst into tears and pulled away. I was uncomfortable and cold, so I put my shirt back on and perched on his bed.

"I'm sorry," he said. "It's not you or your breasts. They're just so different from my wife's."

What the hell? I thought.

"Not in a bad way!" he continued. "Feeling them just reminded me how much I loved … still love, her. I can't do this. I'm sorry."

I gave him a hug, told him not to worry. Then he showed me out.

So, that was it, diary. Three months on this new crazy journey Temple started me on, and I'm in bed with a strange crying man. I need to reassess my situation. Time to shower and go lie in bed with another man who's become a stranger to me. I hope he doesn't cry, too.

Joan Disillusioned-With-Love Colderman

Authors

Rachel Ambrose is a twenty-something fiction writer from Connecticut. Her favorite season is winter, she enjoys well-made Manhattans, and she loves Southern fiction. Her work has appeared in *Crack the Spine*, *Exiles Literary Magazine*, and *The Colton Review*. Currently at work on her second novel, she blogs at http://victorywhiskeyjuliet.tumblr.com.

Lynn Beighley is a fiction writer stuck in a technical book writer's body. Her stories often involve deeply flawed characters and the unsatisfying meshing of the virtual and actual world. She has an MFA in Creative Writing and currently has 16 books published.

Margaret Bingel is just a writer, living in Manchester, New Hampshire. She spends her time working at her father's beer store, art modeling, and writing (when she can). She doesn't have a website or a blog yet, but who knows, maybe she'll have one in the future.

Guilie Castillo-Oriard is a Mexican writer currently exiled in the island of Curaçao. She misses Mexican food and Mexican *amabilidad*, but the laissez-faire attitude and the beaches of the Caribbean are fair exchange. Plus, the bounty of cultural diversity inspires great culture-clash fiction. Guilie is currently revising and editing her first novel. Her short stories have appeared in *Fiction 365*, *Lady Ink Magazine* and *Pure Slush*. She blogs at http://guilie-castillo-oriard.blogspot.com.

John Wentworth Chapin lives and writes in Baltimore, where he is too frequently starting Project B before finishing Project A. John writes non-fiction as well as fiction. Find him on the web at http://johnwentworthchapin.com.

James Claffey hails from County Westmeath, Ireland, and lives on an avocado ranch in Carpinteria, CA with his family. He is the author of a collection of short fiction, *Blood a Cold Blue*. His website can be found at http://jamesclaffey.com.

Gay Degani has published online and in print including *The Best of Every Day Fiction* editions and her own collection, *Pomegranate Stories*. She is the founder-editor emeritus of EDF's *Flash Fiction Chronicles*, a staff editor at *Smokelong Quarterly*, and blogs at *Words in Place* where a list of her work can be found. She's had two stories nominated for Pushcart consideration and won the eleventh Annual Glass Woman Prize for her flash piece, *Something about L.A.*

Michelle Elvy is an editor and writer who has meandered from the shores of the Chesapeake to New Zealand's Bay of Islands. Michelle has published poetry, short stories and non-fiction about travel, faraway places, food, motorcycling, slow travel, the kindness of strangers and raising children in unusual places for numerous literary journals and magazines in the US, Canada, Australasia, UK and Europe. She edits at *Flash Frontier: An Adventure in Short Fiction* and *Blue Five Notebook*. She can also be found regularly at *Awkword Paper Cut*. More about manuscript assessment and Michelle's take on editing and writing at http://michelleelvy.com.

Gloria Garfunkel is the daughter of two Auschwitz survivors which deeply affected her whole life and personality. She has a Ph.D. from Harvard University in Psychology and Social Relations, concentrating on Personality Development Studies. She was a psychotherapist for thirty years working with children, adults and families. She is currently retired, reading and writing to her heart's content. She has published many stories in journals and anthologies and hopes to eventually publish a collection of her flash fiction. Find more at her blog http://queruloussquirreldaily.blogspot.com/.

Teresa Burns Gunther has had fiction and non-fiction appear in numerous literary journals and most recently in *Northwind Magazine*, *Bookslut* and *Best New Writing 2012*. Teresa is the Editor of *The Lakeside*, an online literary magazine, and she founded Lakeshore Writers Workshop in Oakland, California where she leads creative writing workshops and classes and works one-on-one with writers. Find her work at http://www.teresaburnsgunther.com/.

Gill Hoffs lives with her family and an ever-dwindling supply of Nutella in the North of England. Find Gill on facebook or as @gillhoffs on twitter, email her a dirty joke at gillhoffs@hotmail.co.uk, or leave a clean comment at http://gillhoffs.wordpress.com/. *Wild: a collection* is out now from *Pure Slush Books*. Her non-fiction book *The Sinking of RMS Tayleur: the Lost Story of the Victorian Titanic* is also out now, from Pen & Sword. (See her site or http://www.pen-and-sword.co.uk/ for details.) Feel free to send her chocolate.

Joanne Jagoda of Oakland, California, took an inspiring writing workshop after retiring in 2009, and launched on a long-postponed creative writing journey. Since discovering her passion for writing, she has worked non-stop on short stories, poetry and non-fiction. Her work has appeared in a number of e-zines and print anthologies, including *Pure Slush* and *Idea Gems Magazine*, and she was a poet of the month for a Jewish news weekly in Northern California. When not taking writing and poetry classes, Joanne enjoys being a writer-coach for ninth graders, Zumba, and visiting her three grandchildren in Jerusalem.

Len Kuntz is a writer from Washington State and an editor at the online literary magazine *Metazen*. His work appears widely in print and online. You can find more of his work at http://lenkuntz.blogspot.com.

Sally-Anne Macomber was born and raised in Toronto, Canada, and studied journalism at Concordia University in Montreal. Her work on high fashion and the demise of haute couture has appeared in various online and print publications in both Europe and North America. She turned to writing flash fiction in 2010, and hasn't looked back.

Jessica McHugh is an author of speculative fiction that spans the genre from horror and alternate history to epic fantasy. A member of the Horror Writers Association and a 2013 Pulp Ark nominee, she has devoted herself to novels, short stories, poetry, and playwriting. Jessica has had thirteen books published in five years, including the bestselling *Rabbits in the Garden*, *The Sky: The World* and the gritty coming-of-age thriller, *PINS*. More info on her speculations and publications can be found at http://www.jessicamchughbooks.com.

Gwendolyn Joyce Mintz is a fiction writer and aspiring photographer. Her work has appeared in various online and print publications. In other incarnations, Mintz is a writing instructor, a teddy bear maker and somebody's grandmother.

h. l. nelson is Founding Editor/Executive Director of *Cease, Cows* lit mag and a former sidewalk mannequin. Pub credits: *PANK, Hobart, Connotation Press, Metazen, Drunk Monkeys, Red Fez, Bartleby Snopes*. She's also editing an anthology which includes stories by Aimee Bender, Roxane Gay, Lindsay Hunter and other fierce women writers. Her MFA is currently kicking her ass. Tell her what you're wearing: heather@hlnelson.com.

Mandy Nicol grew up in Melbourne, Australia and made a tree change to country Victoria in the mid-nineties – the decade, not her age. She has various animals including a flockette of pet sheep that are thankful for her vegaquarian habits. She writes short stories and loves flash fiction. *Pure Slush* is the first venue to publish her work.

Derek Osborne lives in eastern Pennsylvania. His work has appeared in *Boston Literary Magazine*, *Bartleby Snopes*, *Literary Orphans*, *The Linnet's Wings*, *Pure Slush* and many others. To read more visit http://gertrudesflat.blogspot.com, or email him at derekosborne1@gmail.com.

Vanessa Weibler Paris lives in Erie, Pa., with a guy, a girl, a boy, a bunny rabbit and a dog. She writes things both real (for work) and pretend (for fun). Her favorite things include hot peppers, bad puns, small-world stories, and tales with a twist at the end.

Gary Percesepe is Associate Editor at *New World Writing* (formerly *Mississippi Review*) and a Contributor at *The*

Nervous Breakdown. Author of four books in philosophy, Percesepe's poetry, fiction, essays, and interviews have appeared in *Story Quarterly*, *N + 1*, *Salon*, *Mississippi Review*, *The Millions*, *Brevity*, *PANK*, *Metazen*, *The Brooklyner*, and other places. His collection of short stories, *Why I Did the Grocery Girl*, is forthcoming from Aqueous Books. His poetry collection *falling* and his flash fiction collection *itch* were published by *Pure Slush Books* in late 2013. He has taught at Saint Louis University, Wittenberg University, and University of Dayton. He lives in Buffalo, New York.

Matt Potter is an Australian-born writer who keeps a part of his psyche in Berlin. Matt has been published in various places online, and he is, rather amazingly, also the founding editor of *Pure Slush*. You can find more of his work at his website: http://mattcpotter.webs.com/.

Darryl Price was born in Kentucky and educated at Thomas More College. A founding member of L. Jack Roth's Yellow Pages Poets, he has published dozens of chapbooks, and his poems have appeared in many journals. He currently edits *Olentangy Review* with his wife Melissa.

Stephen V. Ramey is an American author from New Castle, Pennsylvania. His work has appeared in many places, including *The Doctor TJ Eckleburg Review*, *The Journal of Compressed Creative Arts*, and *A Capella Zoo*. *Glass Animals*, his first collection of (very) short fiction is available from *Pure Slush Books*. Find him and more of his work at http://www.stephenvramey.com.

Shane Simmons is a self-confessed coffee shop writer who believes that regardless of quality, each paragraph penned should be rewarded with sweet treats (cake, muffins, Belgian waffles, etc). London-born, he ran away to Glasgow ten years ago, expanded his waistline and now blogs at http://scribblingsimmons.wordpress.com/.

Kimberlee Smith is a writer whose poetry, essays, fiction, and creative non-fiction have been published in numerous literary journals and anthologies. She was awarded a residency to the Jentel Arts Program in 2013. She lives with her two daughters, two dogs, three cats, two rabbits, and nine chooks on her farm in rural Connecticut. She received her MA in English from the University of Sydney, a certificate in the Creative Writing Program through UCLA, and her BA in Journalism from the University of Southern California. She is enrolled currently in post-graduate studies at Columbia University in New York. She can do a headstand on a trampoline, kill a chook, and make hard cider from the apples in her orchard.

Andrew Stancek was born in Bratislava and saw Russian tanks occupying his homeland. His dreams of circuses and ice cream, flying and lion-taming, miracle and romance have appeared recently in print in *LA Review*, *Windsor Review* and *New Sun Rising: Stories for Japan*. Among the many online publications featuring his work are *Every Day Fiction*, *Gemini Magazine* (Flash Fiction Contest Grand Prize Winner), *fwriction*, *r.kv.r.y. quarterly literary journal*, *Tin House*, *Flash Fiction* Chronicles, *The Linnet's Wings*, *Connotation Press*, *THIS Literary Magazine*, *LA Review*, *Windsor Review*, *Thrice Fiction Magazine*, *New Sun Rising*, and *Pure Slush*.

Susan Tepper is the author of four published books of fiction and a chapbook of poetry. Her most recent title *The Merrill Diaries* (*Pure Slush Books*, July 2013) is a Novel in Stories that follow a young woman's adventures in love and lust on two continents, spanning a decade. Tepper has received nine Pushcart nominations, and one for the

Pulitzer Prize in fiction. You can visit her website here: http://www.susantepper.com.

Nathaniel Tower lives in the Twin Cities with his wife and daughter. After teaching high school English for nine years, he decided to pursue a career in writing / publishing / editing. His fiction has appeared in over two hundred online and print journals. His first collection of fiction, *Nagging Wives, Foolish Husbands*, was released in 2014 through *Martian Lit*. Nathaniel is the founding and managing editor of *Bartleby Snopes Literary Magazine and Press*. You can find out more about Nathaniel at http://nathanieltower.wordpress.com.

Townsend Walker lives in San Francisco. His stories have been published in over fifty literary journals and included in seven anthologies. One story won the SLO NightWriters story contest. Two were nominated for the PEN / O. Henry Award. Four were performed at the New Short Fiction Series in Hollywood. He is associate editor at *Grey Sparrow Journal*. During a career in finance he published three books, on foreign exchange, derivatives and portfolio management. Educated at Georgetown, NYU and Stanford, his website is at http://www.townsendwalker.com.

Michael Webb is continually surprised anyone is interested in what he has to say, and he blogs occasionally at http://innocentsaccidentshints.blogspot.com.

Other volumes in the *2014* series
from Pure Slush

Visit the Pure Slush Store:
http://pureslush.webs.com/store.htm

May 2014 Vol. 5
ISBN: 978-1-925101-30-0

June 2014 Vol. 6
ISBN: 978-1-925101-49-2

July 2014 Vol. 7
ISBN: 978-1-925101-37-9

September 2014 Vol. 9
ISBN: 978-1-925101-43-0

October 2014 Vol. 10
ISBN: 978-1-925101-50-8

November 2014 Vol. 11
ISBN: 978-1-925101-53-9

www.ingramcontent.com/pod-product-compliance
Lightning Source LLC
Chambersburg PA
CBHW052141170626
46812CB00004B/1534